A
WANDER
~IN THE~
WOODS
2021

Astonishing Adventures

Edited By Roseanna Caswell

First published in Great Britain in 2021 by:

 Young**Writers**®
— Est. 1991 —

Young Writers
Remus House
Coltsfoot Drive
Peterborough
PE2 9BF
Telephone: 01733 890066
Website: www.youngwriters.co.uk

Printed and bound in the UK by BookPrintingUK
Website: www.bookprintinguk.com
YB0472B

FOREWORD

Welcome, Reader!

Are you ready to take a Wander in the Woods? Then come right this way - your journey to amazing adventures awaits. It's very simple, all you have to do is turn the page and you'll be transported into a forest brimming with super stories.

Is it magic? Is it a trick? No! It's all down to the skill and imagination of primary school pupils from around the country. We gave them the task of writing a story and to do it in just 100 words! I think you'll agree they've achieved that brilliantly – this book is jam-packed with exciting and thrilling tales, and such variety too, from mystical portals to creepy monsters lurking in the dark!

These young authors have brought their ideas to life using only their words. This is the power of creativity and it gives us life too! Here at Young Writers we want to pass our love of the written word onto the next generation and what better way to do that than to celebrate their writing by publishing it in a book!

It sets their work free from homework books and notepads and puts it where it deserves to be – out in the world and preserved forever! Each awesome author in this book should be super proud of themselves, and now they've got proof of their ideas and their creativity in black and white, to look back on in years to come!

CONTENTS

Christ Church CE Primary School, Surbiton

Jimmy McGarry (9)	45
Zoe Bruce (9)	46
Violet Bachelor (9)	47
Ben Allen (8)	48
Annabel Brook (9)	49
Jeevan Rai (8)	50
Sofia Mufti (8)	51
Chloe Williams (8)	52
Charlie Piper (8)	53
Arlo Whyte (9)	54
Matty Nixon (9)	55
William Rhodes (9)	56
Alexander Geach (9)	57
Anshu Kachiraju (9)	58
Lilly Elkhalafy (8)	59
Frankie Bossom (8)	60
Aran Kapadia (9)	61
Harry Payne (9)	62
Isabella Davidson (8)	63
Iris Young (9)	64
Chloe Els (9)	65
Jaden Ng (9)	66
Alesia Rotaru (9)	67
Iskren Simeonov (9)	68
Sruthi Suprabha Machiraju (8)	69
Oscar Brewer (9)	70
Amelie Urwin (8)	71

Crocketts Community Primary School, Smethwick

Udhamveer Singh (7)	72
Deena Al Nasri (8)	73
Sukhreet Sandhu (7)	74
Jiarni Salmon (7)	75
Gurseerat Kaur Sahota (8)	76
Manjot Kaur (7)	77
Jasleen Kaur (7)	78
Saryan Takhar (8)	79

Cumnor CE Primary School, Cumnor

Lily Reed (11)	80
Maddie Knowles (11)	81
Micah Castella McDonald (11)	82
Tom Morris (11)	83
Lily Rose (11)	84
Libby Martin (11)	85
Nikita Shchepinov (11)	86
Isla Bell (11)	87
Daisy Franklin (11)	88
Amelia Atkins (10)	89
Jeremy Effah (10)	90
Rosie Roycroft (11)	91
Caleb Poon (11)	92
Sara Curillova (10)	93
Harrison Daci	94
Benjamin Robinson (11)	95

Daneshill School, Hook

Theo Haines (10)	96
Elouisa Preston-Sparrow (10)	97
Saffi Raj (10)	98
Milo Ramage (9)	99
Chloe Guthrie (9)	100
Roselie du Bruyn (10)	101
Riley Moncrieff (10)	102
Poppy Molloy (10)	103
Emily David (10)	104
Miriam Kimber (10)	105
Ted Brownfield (9)	106
James Mason (9)	107
Charlie Downs (10)	108
Leela Chauhan (10)	109
Millie Swarbrick (9)	110
Megan Harrison (9)	111
Kate Hursey (9)	112
Lola Franklin Adams (10)	113
Sammy Langly-Smith (9)	114
Rupert Fitzgerald (10)	115
Stan Britz (10)	116
Mirabelle Selby (9)	117

Lois Hughes (10)   118
Josephine Oliphant (10)   119
Lenny Smith (9)   120
Jasper Crowther (10)   121
Olive Bailey (10)   122
Emma Wheeler (10)   123
John Love (10)   124
Henry Francis (10)   125

Eveline Day School, Tooting

Rahul Mackinlay (10)   126
Stanley Taylor (11)   127
Maria Kostyleva (9)   128
Lili Marley (9)   129
Leo Thomas Brannan (9)   130

GEMS Founders School - Al Mizah, Dubai

Fatimah Khan (8)   131
Yousef Nagi (8)   132
Ali Hamza Hasan Sadiq (8)   133

Lady Royd Primary, Bradford

Rayaan Rauf (9)   134

Lark Hill Community Primary School, Salford

Anu Oyetade (8)   135

Leighswood School, Aldridge

Harry Davies (9)   136
Macie Williams (9)   137

Lenham Primary School, Lenham

Hannah Bradley (9)   138

Martin Wilson School, Castlefields

Oliver Smith (11)   139

Newtonmore Primary School, Newtonmore

Lucie Vis (11)   140

Russells Hall Primary School, Russells Hall Estate

Georgia Bibin (11)   141
Josh Bullock (11)   142
Victoria Jednorog (10)   143
Mckenzie Garland (11)   144

Short Heath Junior School, Willenhall

Kyle Phillips (9)   145

St Aidan's Catholic Primary Academy, Ilford

Munachim Okoliocha (10)   146
Idah Milla Mkandawire (10)   147
Ilham Quddus (10)   148
Luke McMorrow (11)   149
Michelle Okena (10)   150
Liyana Miah (11)   151
Aydin Rahman (11)   152
Dylan Velenia-Magallona (10)   153
Cristiano Fernandes (11)   154
Divya Ashna Beekawoo (11)   155
Arun Jindal (11)   156
Tyra Chikandira (11)   157

St Augustine's Catholic Primary School, Leeds

Theo Melchor Cahilig (8)   158
Sachi Trinidad Go (8)   159
Mujtaba Alizadah (8)   160

Rahmel Maynard (8) — 161
Anna Więckiewicz (8) — 162
Maria Braganza (8) — 163
Nikitha Chelladurai (8) — 164
Isabella Obiri Yeboah (9) — 165

St Bede CE Primary School, Bolton

Liam Fallows (11) — 166
Mazie Ruby Louise Hall (11) — 167

St Bride's Primary School, Belfast

Ellen Kinney (10) — 168

St Luke's CE Primary School, Lambeth

Kalya Musial (11) — 169

Sutton St James Primary School, Sutton St James

Elsie Christine Ellis (10) — 170
Ellis Redden (10) — 171
Kasey Taylor (10) — 172
Ryan Bollons (10) — 173
Kirk Barker (10) — 174
Leon (10) — 175
Leah Barker (11) — 176
Zuzanna Poznaniak (11) — 177
Aaron Martin (10) — 178
Aarav Keshvara (11) — 179
Zac Parker (10) — 180
T B (9) — 181
Elizabeth Norman (9) — 182
Alesha Harrison (11) — 183

Tangmere Primary Academy, Tangmere

Elsie Freegard (11) — 184

The Academy School, Rosslyn Hill

Matvey Avetisyan (8) — 185
Saoirse Leech (8) — 186
Lily Husain (8) — 187

The Bewbush Academy, Bewbush

Romeo Tomlinson (8) — 188
Ella Hoelters (9) — 189
Victoria Dragan (8) — 190
Lilly-Grace Bowden (8) — 191
Sasha Neill (9) — 192

Yattendon School, Horley

Viola Tammaro (8) — 193
Millie Finch (7) — 194
Lily Bartlett (11) — 195
Chloe Pickett (7) — 196
Jake Bardsley (11) & Charlie George (11) — 197
Olivia Harding (10) — 198
Freya Hawley (10) — 199
Madeleine Birch (9) — 200
Ollie Luszczak (7) — 201
Coby Jones (11) — 202
Oliver Challis (8) — 203
Sophia Graham (9) — 204
Caitlin Jobson (10) — 205
Esme Lyon-Lee (10) — 206
Teddy King (8) — 207
Olivia Moore (9) — 208
Sophia Williams (10) — 209
Fleur Hunt (7) — 210
Nicholas Lowes (11) — 211
Bea Millard (10) — 212

THE
STORIES

A Walk Through The Siberian Forest

One snowy morning, a boy came out of a small hut carrying a sled under his arm and a clipboard-sized package. He ran through the forest and came to a snowy hill with a curve leading to a second hill. As he was about to sled down, a Siberian tiger emerged from the other side. Quickly the boy sled down the hill, unwrapped his package and threw it to the tiger who caught it in his mouth (it was a piece of raw meat). The boy sled down the second hill shouting, "Merry Christmas!" as the tiger happily munched away.

Matthew Dobbelmann

American School Of The Hague, The Netherlands

A Wander In The Woods

I'm on holiday with my family; my mum, Nell, my sister and Nana. We're all driving in a beaten-up car. At a specific patch of woods, Nana stops the car. Apparently, she'd like to find a statue.
We hunt through the trees as the sun begins to set and eventually find it. Nana's wrinkled fingers apprehensively caress its hands. Suddenly, her body jerks to the left, then to the right. All her limbs flail in aimless directions, her eyes are hypnotising.
I run and hide. I wait. Footsteps crunch on shrivelled leaves. I close my eyes. I'm going to die...

Isla MacMillan (11)
Avonwood Primary School, Bournemouth

Shoot

The torrid sun launches its rays onto my bare back, a set of maroon arrows rest on my peeling skin. A perpetual silence pervades the eerie forest as the warmth begins to consume me. The trees are too thin to offer much concealment. The woods around me are awfully uninviting.

My attention has been robbed. An acrid smoke contaminates the air. A figure ascends slowly from the fog. I stagger backwards. They haven't caught sight of me yet. I duck down, feeling the gentle incline of the woodland floor. I ready my arrow and directly aim at my assailant. Shoot...

Lucia Frezza (11)

Avonwood Primary School, Bournemouth

Chocolate Home

A young girl was running and skipping through green forests, hiding from everything. Sitting outside their chocolate house were three pigs wallowing happily in mud. Their friend Sparkles began to eat their delicious house. "Stop, Stop! That's our new home!" shouted Matt.
"What's wrong?" asked Sparkles with a mouthful of chocolate. They stared at the large hole in the roof and sobbed. "Use my magical horn, you have three wishes." In a flash, their house was recreated, complete with furniture and party room. Not forgetting the mud patch! They celebrated with pizza, doughnuts and cola, watched by the hidden girl.

Shylah C (11)

Barley Close Community Primary School, Mangotsfield

An 'Innocent' Campfire Story

"Unlike yours, my story's true," I began. A swift, whispered murmur shot all around, even the shady oaks surrounding us consulted how unlikely it was that my 'tale' was true.

"I was hunted!" I continued. "A savage human with bloodstained clothing held me hostage! He was hauling me across a dirt trail when I bit his leg to escape." I hesitated. "I now live a life of secrecy; only visiting welcoming campers when my deep-seated thirst for human flesh becomes unbearable."

The crowd were in stunned silence. I removed my hood, revealing myself. A demon...

"Grubs up," I smirked.

Layla Henson

Barley Close Community Primary School, Mangotsfield

Mysterious Mushroom

Billy ran. He found a ruby mushroom. The mushroom looked shiny. Billy took a huge chunk and ate it in one bite. Billy got dizzy.
Over the tall, towering trees, came a blue bird. He said, "Argh!"
Billy awoke. The bird was singing like Ellie Goulding. Billy thought it was some good singing. "Who is that?"
The bird said, "Are you okay?"
"Yes, I am," said Billy with confusion.
The blue bird was called Jazzy Bird. Jazzy Bird brought some medicine. Billy cried himself to sleep. Jazzy Bird stroked his small head. Jazzy Bird smiled.

Megan Ricketts (10)

Barley Close Community Primary School, Mangotsfield

The Forest Behind

In the dark, withering woods, the sun stayed overhead. I'd always wanted to wander through Still Hide forest. I dragged my friend, Thomas, in with me, without our parents' allowance. We went only metres in, exploring, losing sanity to weird, abnormal noises.

We walked around ten metres further before a rattle came from behind. We turned cautiously. We couldn't even see an exit.

"It can't get worse from here," I said.

But darkness rose in a fury. Thomas and I ran back the way we came, to find nothing. We turned once again and to my surprise, to freedom!

Daniel T (10)
Barley Close Community Primary School, Mangotsfield

Behind The Fog And Mist

I arrived at the rendevous point. We'd discussed that we'd both arrive at 8.17pm sharp, Thursday night. He wasn't here. Why?

Fog and mist devoured my sight. I found my way through it. A cold shiver ran down my spine. With a sudden thump, I fell to the ground. I'd tripped over an ancient skeleton.

As the mist cleared, I saw a forbidden graveyard. There were countless headstones. One caught my eye. I examined it and discovered a blood-covered identification tag. I wiped the debris away and read: 'Jason Brown'. I froze. That was the person I was meeting...

Chloe B (10)
Barley Close Community Primary School, Mangotsfield

The Family Reunion

He had seen the day coming Krystal stomped down the stairs.

"Paul, today you are going to take the children down to the woods and leave them there."

At noon, he took them down to the heart of the woods. He told them he would come back and then he left.

"Hansel," said Gretel in a shaky voice. "Do you think Papa is really coming back for us?"

"I don't know," replied Hansel in an equally shaky voice.

Four days later, as they were giving up hope, their dad emerged. He took them home. Krystal was nowhere to be seen...

Aimee W (11)

Barley Close Community Primary School, Mangotsfield

Goldilocks And The Three Foxes

I'd finally escaped those three bears.

My hunger is growing. I've never felt this hungry. Oh, a picnic! Surely they won't notice one measly loaf of bread is gone? I need to eat this quickly before anyone gets ba-... Oh no! Someone's coming. There are three of them. They won't find me behind this tree. All I have to do is eat this bread and slip away.

I'm louder than I want to be. At least they don't notice me.

"Hey! You stole our bread!"

I've got to get out of here.

Home... but the door looks like it's grown...

Moreno S (10)
Barley Close Community Primary School, Mangotsfield

Escape The Island

I've finally escaped, it's just me, Roth and Becky. It was risky going back there; it was a horrifying sight, seeing my best friend squished to death but now the three of us are back in the woods, safe at last.

Day twenty, we still have no way off this island but we've the resources to make an escape. Suddenly natives, armed with lit torches run towards us. Fire rages and inferno surrounds the woods. We run to safety leaving everything behind. Sensing disaster, the forces of the forest summon a tsunami sweeping away any evidence of my best friend.

Cassius Christie-Paige (11)
Barley Close Community Primary School, Mangotsfield

The Abandoned Sixteen-Year-Old

There I was. Alone. Crying in the middle of these mysterious woodlands. Somebody took me... Where was Mum? Covered in sweat, I awoke suddenly. It was the same dream I'd had for sixteen years. Again I asked my captor why I was imprisoned here. Slowly he crept towards me. His piercing eyes overshadowed me. He stood silently. Finally he spoke. Revealing my past. Horror spread through me. I grabbed my stuff. Night fell. I made my escape and stumbled into the forest. The ripe spring blossoms were growing. Were these the woods where my mum had abandoned me?

Yvie H (11)
Barley Close Community Primary School, Mangotsfield

The Talking Myth

I sat at my window. For years, I'd been wondering what was in the forest. I went downstairs to ask my mother if she'd go and explore it.
"No, it's too dangerous."
I went upstairs.
Years later, I decided to explore when Mum wasn't home. My bunny came too. I stepped into the forest. A shiver ran down my spine. I kept going and I got lost. All of a sudden, there were talking rabbits and other creatures came out.
They said, "If you see the lady, don't look her in her eyes or else... You'll see..."

Macey Heavens (11)

Barley Close Community Primary School, Mangotsfield

The Life Of Being Alone - Mart's Story

It was getting dark. I walked out of my house and entered the forbidden forest.

I saw a path. I went to the soggy, saturated footpath. I saw three trees in a triangular shape. There were some sticks, rocks and leaves.

After a few minutes, I was almost done with my fort. I hopped up and fell asleep.

After a month of not knowing my way home, there were posters saying: 'Mart, 13 years old. Missing'. Then blinding lights were shining through.

"I'm scared," I murmured.

Then a rescue dog ran over and barked...

Thomas B (11)

Barley Close Community Primary School, Mangotsfield

Little Blue Riding Hood

Once upon a time, in a galaxy far away, a girl was on her way to visit her grandma. She decided to take a shortcut through the dark, sinister thicket. She heard a creepy laugh. It got louder and louder. Then it stopped.

She arrived at Grandma's. No one answered. Grandma was missing. There was a knock at the door. There was a beast and a man.

"The beast has eaten Grandma," said the man. They cut open the beast and out came Grandma, alive and healthy. They buried the beast and Grandma was happy that everyone was okay.

Alfie Heavens (11)

Barley Close Community Primary School, Mangotsfield

Amelia And Thomas' Wolfish Escape!

We walked towards a forest we'd never seen before. We arrived in front of the forest. I nagged Thomas to let us enter. Eventually, he agreed. Together, we entered.

We walked further into the forest. I hear da voice behind me. Slowly, I turned around and saw a werewolf! Quickly, the beast grabbed Thomas and ran. I turned my phone on to dial 999 but my battery had died.

I walked steadily followed the wolf's footsteps to find its den. I ran in, grabbed Thomas and ran out. I snatched his phone, dialled 999 and found our way back home.

Veronica Pietek (10)

Barley Close Community Primary School, Mangotsfield

Cave Of Treasure

There was an imaginary girl called Bhavi. She was ready to go on the school trip.

"Bye, Mom!" she said.

She ran to school.

"Okay, children, are you ready to search the cave of treasure?" said the headmistress.

They got started. She and her friend, Maisy, found the cave. But when they went closer, they found two more caves. They went to the first cave and found the treasure. They put it in the bag. Bhavi saw something shining. It was a diamond.

As she was about to touch it, she woke up from her dream...

Bhavika Kasthuri (11)
Barley Close Community Primary School, Mangotsfield

Life-Changing News

In the distance, I saw a shadow coming closer and closer. Dad! Then he went. I was alone in the cold, dark woods.

Loneliness for 13 years. Another lonely birthday. I'm going to find my long-lost dad. The bright golden sun appeared. I set off.

The dark abandoned church stood in front of me. I went inside with the noise of sobbing ringing in my ears. My dad lay dead on the floor. My mum was there and hurried me away into the woods.

Leaves crunched under my paws. I'll never forget you, Dad. As I looked up, opened eyed...

Lanie R (10)

Barley Close Community Primary School, Mangotsfield

The Three Little Mice

Once upon a time, there were three mice called Jack, James and Jim. Their mum was called Jane. She was always telling them about the big bad eagle.

One day, their mum went out to the beautiful valley, but she never returned home. The mice were getting hungry. They went out to face the big bad eagle.

They climbed the enchanted mountain, looking down at the ground. Clambering to get to the top, they tumbled into the mysterious nest. They grabbed their mum and ran.

Home safely, the eagle was gone for good. They were very happy.

Callum S (11)
Barley Close Community Primary School, Mangotsfield

The Waterfall

I was running. I didn't think about it, my legs were just taking me. Thoughts rushed through my head as I stopped. I took shade under a tree, sweat pouring down me.

Suddenly, I heard a rustling in the leaves, twigs snapping. I looked up and bolted through the woods.

I came to a sudden halt. In front of me stood a magnificent waterfall. Something wasn't right. There was a gap in-between the rock and waterfall. I squeezed through. Inside was everything I'd need.

I laid down, hoping that someday I would get home...

Gracie Ellis (10)

Barley Close Community Primary School, Mangotsfield

The Campfire

Wandering in the woods, I heard a noise behind me. Without hesitation, I started sprinting. Even though I assumed it would be my brother, I was petrified. I looked around. A silhouette! The cabin was in sight. Relief washed over me. Yet, as soon as I saw Ben with my mum, that feeling left me. Finally, the door! For a split second, I believed I was safe until I tried the handle. It was locked! Terrified, I shrank to the ground as I felt the figure's shadow loom over me.

Everyone was in awe as I finished my campfire story...

Isobel Mead (10)
Barley Close Community Primary School, Mangotsfield

My 'Innocent' Friend

Misty air from the dull sky filtered through my window. Another day of my mournful life.
My older friend, Ashley, picked me up in her ink red convertible. Black see-through windows blocked the noise of civilians we passed. The trunk held the suitcases full of useless products and the latest designer clothes. My knees jutted up just under my chin as I sat down on the midnight-black leather. Finally, we were there. I had my suspicions but now I knew for sure... she was the killer and I'm her next victim.
Why me?

Scarlett Meek (11)

Barley Close Community Primary School, Mangotsfield

The Foxes

Finally, it was time to go camping.

When we arrived, Mum and Dad went to set up our tent. My sister and I played hide-and-seek. I hid in the most obvious place, behind a tall tree.

It had been an hour and it's getting dark. My sister still hadn't found me. I heard a noise. What was that? I started running. Ouch! I turned to see foxes looking at me.

They said, "Follow me."

I fearful but I kept walking. I saw Mum and Dad. I said thank you to the foxes. They nodded their heads and ran away.

Summer Fenlon (10)

Barley Close Community Primary School, Mangotsfield

Adventure With Steve

I was getting chased by a creature I had been trying to defeat. The Warden. I ran to shelter but this was no shelter. A maze...
I ran until I'd found another beast. A glowing rabbit. I followed it, as it could lead me to my destination. Little did I know it was a spy.
I turned around and the rabbit perished and found The Warden. I panicked and sprinted away.
I set a trap and went to sleep. I woke up to The Warden suffering pain. I flicked the lever and there was the portal to another dimension...

Spencer L (10)

Barley Close Community Primary School, Mangotsfield

Lost In The Woods

My mother put on the TV. There was a report of children going missing in a maze...

I walked into a forbidden forest, carefully sussing my surroundings. Someone was in here with me. But who...? I decided it didn't matter and kept walking.

As I went deeper into the forest, it seemed to turn into a maze. A crunch behind me. I started to run. Faster than I ever had. There was a man in black chasing me. I found a portal... I went through in case the man came.

It was pink! Children too! And candyfloss!

Chloe C (11)

Barley Close Community Primary School, Mangotsfield

Alice In Wonderland, But With A Twist

It was an ordinary day when a little girl was wandering through the forest. A rabbit caught her eye. she followed it as it went down a hole. Obviously, she travelled after it.

She hit the bottom and ended up in a neon room. Everything was upside down. On an ancient table lay a piece of cake, reading: 'Eat me!'

Instantly, she shrank. A beautiful, stunning dress fell on her. A tiny door appeared to which there stood five angels dressed in white.

It was all a loophole to Heaven.

Whitneystarr Woodey (11)

Barley Close Community Primary School, Mangotsfield

The Door...

It was getting dark. Did Mum even care that I was gone? My thought got interrupted by a noise. It was coming from the forbidden forest.
It was black. Was it a dog, or a cow? No. It was a Pegasus, which was very unusual. It had giant wings and a name tag on its neck. It said: 'Raven'. Raven started walking into the bush she had come from. I started following her. A blinding light straight in front of me revealed a door. What on earth was a door doing in the middle of a forest...?

Marcella M (11)
Barley Close Community Primary School, Mangotsfield

A Wander In The Woods

Tommy got a boat and rowed to the island. The boat drifted away. He was on a magic island with mythical creatures.

Tommy made some weapons and he fought some creatures. Tommy heard a loud horn honk in the distance.

He saw something. It was a massive boat. The boat came to help Tommy.

He made it home safely on the enormous boat. His mum and dad were so happy they cried.

"The police are looking for you!" his mum said.

"Tell them to stop!" said Tommy.

Taylor E (10)

Barley Close Community Primary School, Mangotsfield

A Wander In The Woods

It was dark. I'd escaped. The haunted house was behind me. All I could do was run. I wasn't thinking. I had butterflies in my stomach.

Soon after, I came to a halt. The wind blew. In front of me was a gloomy graveyard. I had to get out. I ran in the direction in front of me, but the wind was strong. It blew me down a hole. I drifted off to sleep...

I woke up. It was morning. I saw the gleaming light through the trees. I ran into the distance, never to go back again.

Georgia A (11)
Barley Close Community Primary School, Mangotsfield

The Bloodthirsty Horror

I was running for my endangered life. I sat down, out of breath. I heard a deep growl behind me. I got up and ran. Lifting some leaves from the ground, I found an escape!

I saw a damaged plane. The stunning birds and trees were being destroyed behind me. I got on the plane and escaped.

The spino grabbed the plane's wing and pulled it down. Then I heard a helicopter. I ran for my life while they called for me.

Then I got to safety. I was saved!

Max B (10)
Barley Close Community Primary School, Mangotsfield

The Secret Wolf!

It all began one dark night in the forest. I was woken up by a loud noise. There was someone coming.

In the distance, I could see some hunters with their guns. I started running until I fell down a hole. With ears were down and tail wagging, a wolf, like me, helped me up. That's when I saw wolves gathering together. I thought I was the only wolf left since my pack was gone. That's when I decided to stay here with them to be safe...

Sasha Mitchell (11)

Barley Close Community Primary School, Mangotsfield

A Mysterious Fire

Waking up in shock, rushing out of bed and down the stairs, I heard a scream. It sounded like a kid. I looked out of the window. The fog was thick but I could see a child running. Suddenly, a fire started next to my cabin. I had to get to the child and my family.

I picked up the child in my tired arms and ran towards safety.

I will never ever forget that night...

Alexia Bradfield (11)

Barley Close Community Primary School, Mangotsfield

Call To The Gods

A girl called Maddy, was 18. Maddy wasn't an ordinary girl. Maddy could fly, turn invisible and had X-ray vision! Maddy lived in a rich mansion with her dog, Charlotte.

One day, Maddy was practising turning invisible and X-ray vision. Suddenly, her strength weakened and she felt them slipping away! Knowing what to do, she calmly drew a chalk circle on the floor to summon the gods.

She shouted, "Asreath metrion sinthos!"

With a strike of lightning, a glowing sphere appeared. Boldly, the girl stepped in...

Florence Patterson (9)

Belmont School, Holmbury St Mary

Francesca's Great Adventure

Suddenly, Francesca's ring started to glow. Out of nowhere, she was taken into a whole new world. There were fairies, pixies, elves and toadstools. Amazingly, some of the fairies were the size of grapes and some of the fairies were the size of bugs.

In the distance, she saw a huge tree. All the animals were crowding around it as if it was a magic tree. Francesca couldn't believe her eyes. Suddenly, she started worrying about how she'd get home.

She went to explore and saw the tree pouring with sweets!

Georgina McLaren (8)

Belmont School, Holmbury St Mary

The Night Of The Bubble-Blowers

It was getting dark as I walked home. I saw an explosion of light in the woods. I wandered in to look and had the shock of my life. I saw a glowing blue UFO.

As I approached, I was immediately blown into a bubble and floated up into the sky. I travelled miles on the breeze. Suddenly, the wind changed direction. Drifting back towards the woods, my bubble caught on a branch. *Pop!*

I scrambled home as quickly as I could. Lying in bed exhausted, I tried to make sense of what I'd seen. Was it all a dream?

Hannah Hooks (8)
Belmont School, Holmbury St Mary

Policeman Joe

Once upon a time, there lived a boy called Joe. Joe lived with his mummy, daddy, brother, Sam and his two grandmas, Oma and Mamma. He also had one black and one golden-coloured dog.

One day, a thief stole one of his dogs. Joe told Oma, who was in the undercover police. She promised to deal with the thief.

Soon, Oma caught the thief and took him to prison.

When Joe got his dog back, he decided he wanted to be a policeman. He trained his dogs to help him. Joe caught many other thieves in his life.

Samuel Ellis (9)
Belmont School, Holmbury St Mary

Mysterious Encounter

There was an enormous jet-black beast with blood-red eyes, his teeth were as sharp as knives and he had drool coming out of his mouth. He hadn't seen me yet. I started stepping backwards to try to get away, but I stood on the loudest twig known to man.

My heart stopped beating. I stopped breathing. The beast stared at me. We were locked in the most bizarre staring competition. Neither of us wanted to look away first.

I was petrified, but he was more frightened than I was. But frightened of what?

Luella Pickup (9)
Belmont School, Holmbury St Mary

Night-Time Wanders

Crash! Bang! Wallop!
Moz and Edgar tried to lift up my head but accidentally dropped it. With me still asleep, they tried again to get Bully, my bulldog pillow, out from under my head.
Finally, they managed to get Bully out and locked him onto the parachute. They struggled to get the window open but they got there in the end and pushed Bully out.
Bully went on a two-hour expedition but he came back just before I awoke.
When I woke up everyone was there.

Millie Guthrie (9)
Belmont School, Holmbury St Mary

Lost In The Forest

It was a dark night. I was investigating a creepy forest. I came across a house. Wait a minute, I've heard rumours about this house... it was haunted. At first, I didn't want to go in, but I knew I had to. When I was in the house, I heard a noise in the kitchen. I went to check it out. When I was looking around, a portal sucked me in.

When I woke up, I was lost in a forest! I started to build a hut.

I'm still here now!

Zi Sian Beh (8)

Blaengarw Primary School, Blaengarw

The Fight

Once there was a fox and a blue bird. They were fighting over a mushroom house.

Fox said, "I'm going to win!"

"No! I am!"

Fox and Blue did some challenges.

Blue said, "How many sit-ups can you do in a minute?"

"Yes, I won!" said Fox.

"Wow!" said Blue.

"I get the house!" said Fox.

But then he felt bad.

He shouted, "Come back. I won't hurt you."

"Why?" said Blue.

"I want you to live with me," said Fox.

Fox and Blue became friends. They laughed and played rock, paper, scissors and tic tac toe.

Molly Jeffels (9)

Brompton & Sawdon Community Primary School, Brompton

The Mysterious Door

There must be a way out, thought Jake. He was trapped inside a never-ending glowing hallway. Jake could see about 100 doors from where he stood. They weren't normal doors, they looked like portals that could zap you through to another world at any moment. Jake couldn't remember how he got there, just that he saw a flash of light. Turning around, Jake saw a huge door.
"This must be the way I came in. If I go back through, I might go home."
Jake took a deep breath and jumped through...

Alannah Ghorst (11)

Brompton & Sawdon Community Primary School, Brompton

How The Thestral Turned Bad

One gloomy night, every creature was asleep, except one, an evil thestral called Nightmare. He was black with evil with red devil eyes.

You may ask how he turned bad. I will tell you. When he was a foal, he was attacked and his mother was shot trying to save him. He has always been vicious and bad and he was scared of humans.

He wanted revenge. He did so by hunting humans like he was hunted when he was little.

So, don't go out at night or Nightmare might come for you!

Orla Kerins (10)

Brompton & Sawdon Community Primary School, Brompton

Midnight

A boy was completely lost in the fog surrounded by forest and wilderness.

"There must be a way out," he said. "Hello? Hello? Is there anyone else here?"

No one knew he was there. He decided to search for a way out.

He searched everywhere but he couldn't find anyone there or a way out. He tried to dig his way out but that didn't work either.

He decided to give up. Then he remembered he still had his phone, so he called for help.

Lola Oxley-Davis (8)

Brompton & Sawdon Community Primary School, Brompton

The Secret Meeting

I got to the secret meeting. My boss showed me my workspace, where I would be working on a project for him.

After two hours of working on the project, I took the sim to him. He did something unexpected. He put a blindfold on me and took me into a locked room. Then he called out his snake.

He said, "If you don't give me the sim, I will feed you to my snake."

I gave him the sim, but there was nothing on it because I hadn't done the work...

Caitlin Harper (11)
Brompton & Sawdon Community Primary School, Brompton

The Sounds Following Me

As darkness fell, the trees loomed over me. The leaves rustling sent a chill down my back. As I continued wandering in the woods, the moon rose higher and the shadows grew bigger.

As my heart pumped faster and a frightened look grew on my face, the sounds followed me through the woods.

While I crept through the woods, I heard growls behind me. I started to up my pace to try to lose track of the growls. Suddenly, it stopped.

As I ran through the woods, another sound followed me. Screams! What a nightmare!

"Jimmy! Breakfast!" my mum shouted...

Jimmy McGarry (9)
Christ Church CE Primary School, Surbiton

Hide-And-Seek

Anna and Elenor loved playing hide-and-seek. It had been their favourite game since nursery. They were both very good at it and enjoyed exploring as they played. The woods were the best place to play - there were thick bushes, tall trees, dark caves and creeping vines. Elenor counted and Anna hid. But that was fifteen minutes ago and Anna was still missing! Elenor had looked in all their usual hiding places and was now beginning to worry. A shiver crawled down her back. Where was Anna? She heard a noise...

"Found you!" shouted Elenor. But was it Anna?

Zoe Bruce (9)

Christ Church CE Primary School, Surbiton

Adventure In The Woods

I awoke in a bed of leaves. I stood up in damp leaf mush. I heard a rustling noise behind me.
It whispered, "Animal villain be gone!"
Was it talking to me? I was about to find out...
I walked along a muddy path and came to a clearing. There was a wolf. It looked like it was expecting me. Surprisingly, it talked to me. It was a magical wolf.
It said, "I must fight you."
It charged towards me. I said the first thing that popped into my head.
"Animal villain be gone!"
The black, villainous wolf was lifeless.

Violet Bachelor (9)
Christ Church CE Primary School, Surbiton

The Haunted House

Following the instructions left for him on a mysterious note he found hidden in his trousers, Bob stumbled through the woods towards the creepy castle.

Behind him, he heard a twig snap. He turned around as quick as a flash and saw a witch out of the corner of his eye. He was petrified.

If I carry on slowly, the witch might not know I noticed her, he thought to himself. The deeper he got into the woods, the more eyes he felt on him. He quickened his step and finally reached the castle.

"Surprise! Happy Halloween!" his friends shouted.

Ben Allen (8)
Christ Church CE Primary School, Surbiton

Cookie Crumbs

As dawn crawled through the darkness, Harry and Grace held on tightly to each other. The twins felt lost and alone. How would they get home?
Their tummies rumbled. Harry looked at the cookie in his hand. Even though they were starving, they had to carry on using its crumbs for the trail, to help them find their way out of the woods.
Just as they were beginning to lose hope, Grace spotted a house that looked like it was made out of ice cream. What was it?
They crept inside and stood open-mouthed.
"Surprise! Happy birthday!" their friends shouted.

Annabel Brook (9)

Christ Church CE Primary School, Surbiton

The Woods

A young boy, called Jeevan, was taking a stroll through the woods. He got lost. Jeevan saw a man. He wondered if he should go up to the man.
But the man was fake. He took off his costume... he was a vampire. The vampire was holding a bloody dead man.
"Argh!"
Jeevan sprinted, but the vampire saw him in the corner of his eye. Jeevan ran. He was sweating. Jeevan got home. He heard a crash! The vampire appeared. He gave Jeevan blood tea. Jeevan was confused. It turned out the horrible vampire that chased him was actually good!

Jeevan Rai (8)
Christ Church CE Primary School, Surbiton

A New Generation Of Cinderella

Cinderella Junior was packing her stuff when she saw a glowing light. She finished packing her things so she could go camping. She ran into the woods to where the light was. It was her mother's fairy godmother.

The fairy godmother led Cinderella Junior to her mother's castle and ripped off her dress. She was a witch! Cinderella Junior screamed.

Sixty years ago, Cinderella Junior grandma had some pretty mean laser eyes which meant that Cinderella Junior had powers too. She suddenly remembered! She used her laser eyes to kill the witch!

Sofia Mufti (8)

Christ Church CE Primary School, Surbiton

Zombie Problem

There was a red glowing eyed hovering zombie. It came flying straight towards me. I ran for my life. It pushed down trees. It came straight for me. I couldn't move. I was petrified.

Suddenly, I got to the cliff nearby. I looked around. I saw a cave. Finally, a place to stay., I ran straight to the cave before the zombie could see me. Suddenly, zombies appeared everywhere. I couldn't escape. *Crack!* I looked behind me. More zombies were behind me. I ran but the zombies followed me. One touched me in the blink of an eye...

Chloe Williams (8)

Christ Church CE Primary School, Surbiton

The Boy In The Forest

I heard rustling leaves behind me. I thought I was alone. I turned around and saw my teacher skulking through the secret forest towards a creepy old oak tree that I'd never noticed before. Weirdly, he seemed to disappear into it.

I decided to follow him. I crept up to the oak with its long twisted branches. I reached out to touch the rough bark. It was then I noticed what looked like a door slightly ajar. A million questions raced through my head. Where did the door lead to? Why was Mr Mars here?

I hesitated before stepping in...

Charlie Piper (8)
Christ Church CE Primary School, Surbiton

The Mystery Mist

I'm the only person still living to tell a tale like this...

I was going for a wander in the woods when, in the distance, I saw some purple fog. I ran towards it. Once I'd reached the mysterious mist, it spoke!

"You sent me to labour," creepily called the unknown voice.

Questions buzzed through my head but before I could say anything, the fog had vanished. I was so confused.

Someone was running towards me. It was an angry prisoner! When he reached me, his jaw dropped. I saw a shadow figure and ran...

Arlo Whyte (9)
Christ Church CE Primary School, Surbiton

The Scary Monster

Yesterday, something terrible happened. A vicious monster was chasing me.

We were running through the thick trees. I stumbled over a tree branch and fell through a hole. I had fallen into an underground cave with beautiful crystals.

I realised the monster was still with me so I looked for an exit. I could see one, but a boulder was blocking it. I stamped down on the floor and the boulder rolled away. I quickly climbed out and hid behind a bush until the monster thought I was gone.

The scary, vicious monster was gone... for now.

Matty Nixon (9)
Christ Church CE Primary School, Surbiton

A Horrific Journey

Yesterday, something terrible happened. I'm the only human who survived to tell this tale...

An army of meteors came to destroy Earth. Tears welled in my eyes. My family blasted me off in an escape pod, into outer space.

As soon as I'd left the Earth's atmosphere, the meteors eliminated Earth. They started to take off but one of them noticed me.

The chase was on. I zoomed off to an unknown green planet. My pod crash-landed. I flew out of the pod and landed in green goo. I got up and saw another army...

William Rhodes (9)
Christ Church CE Primary School, Surbiton

Wander Into The Woods

In the enormous woods, under the light of the full moon, I shivered. As I walked along, feeling scared and alone, the noises of the forest startled me. Was that an owl hooting or a wolf howling? The sound of the wind whistling through the leafless trees heightened my fear.

As the trees swayed in the wind, it felt like the branches were grabbing at me. I pulled my scarlet coat tight and quickened my step. It felt as though all the eyes of the forest were on me. As I crept around the corner, I saw it... Grandpa's house.

Alexander Geach (9)

Christ Church CE Primary School, Surbiton

Happy Halloween Surprise

I have experienced the funniest thing. This is what happened.

I was going to school on my bike. Suddenly, I fell over. I checked if everything was alright. In the corner of my eye, I saw a man with a black eye patch. He was holding a sharp, pointy, shiny sword. I asked who he was. The pirate didn't respond. He put a blindfold over my eyes.

He took me to the woods and into a room. It was filled with people. All of them were dressed up in unusual, scary and extraordinary clothes.

It was a Halloween surprise!

Anshu Kachiraju (9)
Christ Church CE Primary School, Surbiton

Underground House

One night, Megan was still awake. She gazed out of the window and saw black, as usual. She saw something... a light in the woods.

She crept outside to have a look. She was a bit scared to go into the woods, but she went. As she was walking, she fell into a hole. It took her underground.

At the bottom, there was a house. Megan went in. There were people. Megan said hello and they started talking. They showed Megan around and they became friends.

As morning came, Megan had to leave. She told absolutely nobody!

Lilly Elkhalafy (8)

Christ Church CE Primary School, Surbiton

Where In The Woods Will I Go?

Five long, exciting years ago, as the moon awoke, I crept outside to take a wander in the woods. I saw a light glowing in the distance. I went closer and wanted to know what it was... It sucked me inside. In the lonely, unknown darkness, I gathered my courage to keep going. Crazily, I saw a nocturnal town... completely awake in the middle of the night. People, well, when I say people, I mean dwarves, everywhere! Deep down, it felt like home because I'm tiny! Everyone was so kind. It was like a dream of a lifetime.

Frankie Bossom (8)
Christ Church CE Primary School, Surbiton

A Wander In The Woods

I am Bob and I'm in the woods. Behind me is a criminal that's after me. You see, I put this guy in jail about five times and now he's running after me in the woods.

Oh no! He's right there!

I climb up a tree. He's right on my tail. I jump in the water. He's behind me.

Swim! Tread! Trip! Swim! Tread! Trip!

I get out of the water and climb up a big oak tree. I look behind me. He's not there. But then I see him dead with a shadow beast figure standing over him...

Aran Kapadia (9)

Christ Church CE Primary School, Surbiton

Fighting In A Forest

One terrifying day, I heard something coming from the gloomy tree. I looked out of my tent and saw a monster party!

They saw me immediately. I ran. I knew if I got caught I was dead. Annoyingly, the monsters knew I hated homework club so they cornered me. I had nowhere to go. I'd have to do homework. I found a sword and killed them.

After the FBI, the monsters' friends, found out, they pulled out their guns but I used my karate skill to knock them out.

I returned back to where we were camping.

Harry Payne (9)
Christ Church CE Primary School, Surbiton

A Wander In The Woods

Tom lived with his mum and dad on the edge of a deep, dark forest.

One fateful day, Tom took a wander in the forest. He stood outside looking in. Tom took one small step into the forest. He was terrified but he did it. After a while, Tom heard a noise under a pile of leaves. Tom started to run. He rushed back. Tom stopped and turned around but there was nothing there. Tom decided to start walking home.

On his way back, he thought about what had happened. Tom was never ever going into the forest again.

Isabella Davidson (8)

Christ Church CE Primary School, Surbiton

The Spy And The Graveyard

I found my house safely.

I'm the first to live to tell this tale. Yesterday, something terrible happened.

I found an overgrown temple. Then I found a spy. Why was he here? He told me to go to the graveyard.

I went to the graveyard. There was a ghost. I ran for my life, not noticing a big bump. It was a treasure chest. I picked it up and ran into the woods. I wandered through the creepy trees and found a squirrel, bunny, hedgehog and, I think I might have imagined it, but maybe a fairy...

Iris Young (9)

Christ Church CE Primary School, Surbiton

Mysterious Woods Escape

I was going walking in the woods. Mum dropped me off.

I stepped into the woods and turned around to say goodbye... All I could see was the dark forest. I ran and ran, but not a soul was around.

Just then, I heard voices. Maybe not human voices, but I heard something! I followed the sound, then stopped dead in my tracks. Something snapped behind me. I rushed through the woods. I turned around... it was a goblin!

I ran. The path was rocky but I made it! I was out of the woods... or was I?

Chloe Els (9)

Christ Church CE Primary School, Surbiton

Walk In The Woods

One day, a boy went camping. When he was sleeping, he heard a loud noise.

He woke up and went outside. Suddenly, a giant spooky tree was in front of him. He was scared. Abruptly, everything turned real. The tree grabbed him with its branches.

Back at camp, his doll turned big, as big as him. His toy police car turned into a real car. His dolls got in the car with axes.

When the dolls arrived, five of them got out of the car to chop the spooky tree down. The rest of the dolls saved him.

Jaden Ng (9)
Christ Church CE Primary School, Surbiton

The Legend Of The Old Man

It all happened on the night of the sleepover when we decided to go for a walk. Somehow, we ended up in the woods our parents had always told us to stay away from. The Legend of the Old Man kept many people away. Walking through the woods, with the strange shadows and noises, we felt scared. We heard crying, which grew louder with each step. It was an old man. He beckoned us over... We helped him and he was thankful. We are lucky to visit him from time to time and he is always pleased to see us.

Alesia Rotaru (9)

Christ Church CE Primary School, Surbiton

The Monster Surprise

Yesterday, I found a monster!
I trailed my teacher into the deep, gloomy, mysterious woods. My teacher was helping the creepy creatures. I wonder why?
She turned around and nearly saw me. Thank goodness, she didn't see me hiding behind the trees. My teacher was having a party with some skunks. I just couldn't believe my eyes. Was this a dream?
The monsters could feel my blood and fear. The monsters would eat me. Shall I sprint away or shall I keep trailing my teacher...?

Iskren Simeonov (9)
Christ Church CE Primary School, Surbiton

The Enchanted Woods

Something was making the trees fall down. I ran for my life. I tried to get closer and closer. It was a zombie. It came out from the woods. It felt friendly. After a few seconds, red eyes appeared. I couldn't see. This amazed me. It was as bright as the sun. I went closer and closer. The red eyes ran away into the deep, dark forest. I raced to the red eyes. After a bit, the red eyes disappeared. I didn't know what to do. I raced along and found my best friend.

Sruthi Suprabha Machiraju (8)
Christ Church CE Primary School, Surbiton

A Stroll Into The Forest

Once, in a gloomy forest, there was a stroller called Mrs Pearce. She loved the forest. She saw a bush. A boy appeared from the bush. His name was Edward.
The next day, they ran as fast as they could. Edward sacrificed his life for Mrs Pearce and since that day, the forest was called Edward. Mrs Pearce was disappointed because Edward died because of a monstrous tree.
Mrs Pearce remembered Edward's last words, "You go, you must. I will hold it off..."

Oscar Brewer (9)

Christ Church CE Primary School, Surbiton

I Ran Into The Woods

I ran as fast as my little legs could take me. I didn't know if I was going to make it. I ran into the wood. My heart was pumping. Suddenly, all I saw was big black fuzz. I began to feel dizzy. *Bang!* All I remember was seeing a big, dark shadow.
I woke up. I knew that there was no time to lose. I ran. I could see it in the distance. I sped up. We were neck and neck. I ran up the hill.
I made it to the giant cookie! Yay!

Amelie Urwin (8)
Christ Church CE Primary School, Surbiton

The Hidden Forest

A few days ago, some explorers reached a forest called The Hidden Woods. They saw a sign saying: *Do Not Enter!* Everyone was brave and went into the forest.

When they went in, a lava demon started attacking them but they dodged it. Someone found a mountain and called the others over.

The explorer said, "This big mountain just spoke. It will help if you throw water balls at the lava demon."

The explorers killed the lava demon. All the darkness in the forest disappeared and the mountain was free!

Udhamveer Singh (7)

Crocketts Community Primary School, Smethwick

A Small Dog Lost In The Woods

Once upon a time, I arrived somewhere. It was dark. I was scared! Then the lights turned on. I was happy. Then I saw a magical pathway to get home, but the door trapped me!

I got lost in a dark, dark forest. I couldn't see anything except a small dog. It saved me! It was lost, like me.

Both of us were now safe. I named the dog Lily because she was a girl. The dog took me somewhere safe. I was so happy.

We lived together and we were happy together every single day.

Deena Al Nasri (8)
Crocketts Community Primary School, Smethwick

The Magical Forest

It was getting dark and I was lost. I heard something in the bushes. It was a fairy. She was lost too. Two more came. They were also lost. We all needed to work as a team.

"Are we there yet?" asked one fairy.

"No, not yet," the smart one said.

"Is that a dragon?"

We all ran as fast as we could away from the dragon.

"What is this place?" I asked.

"We found it! It's our home!" said the fairies.

Sukhreet Sandhu (7)

Crocketts Community Primary School, Smethwick

74

A Haunted House With Ghosts

I arrived at the secret meeting place. I heard a noise in the bush, It was a ghost!

He scared me into a cage. Lots of bats were flying around me. I tried to figure out how to get out of the cage.

Sunset came and I found a key. I tried the lock on the cage. I was free! Wait! I had to try to get out of there. I kept walking straight. There must be a way out! I kept walking. I still couldn't find the way out. I was scared.

I finally found the way out.

Jiarni Salmon (7)
Crocketts Community Primary School, Smethwick

Walking In The Woods

The Devil Ghost was frightening the animals. The legend was not happy. The legend walked into the woods. She was confused, why were the animals running? They started fighting.

The ghost had 10,000 ghosts to protect him.

"We need to kill the ghost," said the legend.

The legend turned into a ghost. She got close to the Devil Ghost and shot her power at him. The Devil Ghost was defeated. The animals were happy and lived happily ever after.

Gurseerat Kaur Sahota (8)

Crocketts Community Primary School, Smethwick

Dragon World

Once upon a time, there was a little dragon called Frosty. She was a kind dragon that lived in the icy cave in the forest.

One day, there was another dragon that came into the forest. Frosty began fighting with the dragon but then they stopped.

Frosty noticed a symbol on the dragon that her mom had and she had been lost in the woods. She realised the dragon was her mom. She hugged her mom and they lived happily ever after.

Manjot Kaur (7)

Crocketts Community Primary School, Smethwick

The Girl And The Dog

In the dark, horrifying woods was a huge monster. It chased me around the forest but I got away. There was a magic door that needed a magic key. I went searching the forest but still no key.
I was afraid and lonely until a cute dog ran up to me. Then the dog and I went searching the forest together.
It took forever but we finally found the key. We tried it on the door and it worked!

Jasleen Kaur (7)
Crocketts Community Primary School, Smethwick

Ghost Place

Once upon a time, there was a family that went to the forest. All the trees shook and a ghost put them into a cage. There was a puzzle.
They solved it and they escaped the cage. They ended up in a place that was unknown. A noise was coming from a room. They got scared and they went back to the woods, but they got trapped...

Saryan Takhar (8)
Crocketts Community Primary School, Smethwick

Miss Helpful

It was getting dark. I was wandering in the woods, gazing up at the beautiful shining stars. *Crack!* I turned around and studied the mysterious trees. I saw something shining in front of me. It was a fairy.

"Hello," she said in a squeaky voice.

"We need your help!" shouted another fairy from the back of the group.

"Okay," I replied.

They aggressively pulled me and shoved me down a tree stump.

They said, "Can you fix our houses?"

I tried wriggling free but I couldn't.

After a few hours, I was done fixing their tiny houses and went home.

Lily Reed (11)
Cumnor CE Primary School, Cumnor

Homework Club

End of school. Oh! It's homework club. Thursdays are the day I dread. Can't I just do it at home? I'm tired of this. I ran out of the classroom. I dashed out the massive, heavy doors. Wait, what? I'm outside school but in the woods! I looked behind me and the school had vanished.
I ran around for a bit but that just wasted my energy. I kept hearing whispering.
"Join us..."
I was scared. Someone nudged me.
"Maddie! Maddie!" my teacher said.
"You've been daydreaming! Your page is completely blank! Get to work!"

Maddie Knowles (11)
Cumnor CE Primary School, Cumnor

The Lucky Escape?

Run! The one word racing through my head: run! Chest heaving, I furiously wove through the towering trunks, dodging arrows and judging how far the yelling voices were behind me. Taking short, rapid, laboured breaths, I fumbled arrows into my bow and started to randomly fire.

Suddenly, I was all alone. Roots pushed through the undergrowth forming a mighty wall. I let the air flood into my lungs, so exhausted that I didn't notice the roots wrapping around my body with a grip of steel. Struggling wildly, I broke free, leaping down into watery depths appearing below.

Micah Castella McDonald (11)

Cumnor CE Primary School, Cumnor

Lost

Jimmy was lost in the woods. He heard loud footsteps walking in his direction. Jimmy started shaking, then ran. The footsteps kept getting closer and louder. He dared to look back. Nothing was there. The footsteps had stopped.

Jimmy looked back, confused. *Snap!* He jumped in fright. Then he saw something. He was no longer interested in the noise. Something was moving in the distance. It kept getting closer. Then he saw it, a man.

It took five seconds, The man grabbed Jimmy by the shoulder and pulled him away.

Jimmy was never seen again...

Tom Morris (11)
Cumnor CE Primary School, Cumnor

Prisoner 101

I'd escaped... or had I? Guns sounded in my ears. No, I hadn't...

"Where is she? Prisoner 101?" a low voice boomed.

I stumbled over a root, making a loud crack. Looking up, I saw a bush of berries. I hadn't eaten for three days but there was no time to stop now. Suddenly, three guards surrounded me. I was trapped. *Bang!* I fell to the ground. I knew this was the end.

What? I'm alive? I opened my eyes slowly. I was in a purple room, like an office. One word, I saw clearly, on a big sign: 'AFTERLIFE'.

Lily Rose (11)
Cumnor CE Primary School, Cumnor

The Dare Game!

It was my turn... I flinched as Hailey thought of my dare. She then said the dare. I had to go to the forbidden part of the forest.

As I jogged gingerly, I heard a sudden crack. A white face appeared, then disappeared...

I strode on, building up my courage. I eventually found a grey, lifeless graveyard. This was going too far!

I tried to run but I suddenly tumbled into a grave with a blood-splattered tree.

"Gabby!"

It was my friend. She hauled me out and the police roped the graveyard off.

Meanwhile, I sprinted home!

Libby Martin (11)
Cumnor CE Primary School, Cumnor

Hide-And-Seek

The footsteps intensified. I could almost smell the breath of the madman behind me. Twigs crunched under my shoes. My only thought was to get to the secret den.

The trees parted and I was running through a moonlit clearing. I dared to look over my shoulder to check. Yep. He was still running, knife glinting like molten silver.

The trees began closing in again and I was back in the forest. The den appeared and I leapt in, listening to the footsteps fading away.

On the floor lay a biscuit tin. I opened it and indulged in crumbly shortbread.

Nikita Shchepinov (11)
Cumnor CE Primary School, Cumnor

The Red Mushroom

The sun was setting and I was still completely lost after being transported here by a red mushroom. After about three hours of walking, I spotted an alleyway with rickety houses along the sides. I went inside each of them to get help but they were all empty.

Suddenly, I spotted a sign for a maze, so I went inside. There was something mysterious about the maze so I ran quickly. I saw a ghostly white figure in front of me. I screamed in fear and ran in the opposite direction.

"Yes!"

I'd found the familiar red mushroom.

Isla Bell (11)

Cumnor CE Primary School, Cumnor

Can You Keep A Secret?

I'd just remembered, my phone was spamming and I was packing faster than ever.

"Bye, Mom," I said laughing and looking down at my phone.

As we arrived, my friends and I sat on the prickly leaves and began. A dash of pepper, a little bit of dirt and a pinch of salt. We all burst out laughing! Suddenly, a tall, dark and gaunt man circles the trees around us. We felt sudden regret and fear. We got up as quick as a flash and ran to the front gate.

Jess screamed. "Argh!"

Bang! She was gone...

Daisy Franklin (11)
Cumnor CE Primary School, Cumnor

The Escape!

We'd escaped! We ran through the woods, past the old pile of junk and up the rope into the treehouse. I was shocked! I'd just escaped from school with Jake, my best friend. All because of stupid maths and detention, of course. We'd already got two detentions and it wasn't even lunchtime! My mum is sure to kill me!

I got out my lunchbox and started munching through my food. Jake got his food out too. Wait! I heard something rustle. Someone had followed us. I saw Jake stop eating. He'd heard it too. We were doomed!

Amelia Atkins (10)
Cumnor CE Primary School, Cumnor

Stuck In The Woods

It was getting dark. Joe and I were trying to find a way out.

We were playing 'it' in the woods when we were kidnapped. We managed to escape and ran across the deep, sketchy woods. We ran and ran until we almost collapsed. We had no food, no water, no nothing.

After a few hours of rest, Joe suggested we sleep. I agreed as I was tired.

The next morning, we started again. We ran and ran and ran. Then Joe saw something.

"A gate!" he said. "A gate, an exit!"

Or was it...

Jeremy Effah (10)
Cumnor CE Primary School, Cumnor

Fire! Blood!

It was getting dark. I was starting to think there was no way out. Thirsty, cold. Leaves on trees collected rain. Somehow, a raindrop found its way down my spine, making me shiver. I saw a muddy-looking puddle. Do I dare? Do I dare drink some? From the reflection of the puddle, I saw in my eyes... fire! I looked up and immediately ran in the opposite direction.

I was far enough away from the fire to rest. I coughed in my hands... blood! I fell and blacked out...

I opened my eyes. I was back in bed...

Rosie Roycroft (11)
Cumnor CE Primary School, Cumnor

The Trap That Never Fails

Finally, I thought, as I spotted the smoke in the sky.
We have to be close to the hotel.
My new friend, Luke, and I had been hiking for hours and the sun was setting rapidly. We hadn't eaten for a long time.
As we approached the clearing, I realised the smoke was actually coming from a big, old mansion in the middle of nowhere.
When we went in, the door slammed shut behind us. Luke suddenly became a werewolf and a whole pack appeared around me! How would I escape?

Caleb Poon (11)

Cumnor CE Primary School, Cumnor

Gone Forever

We arrived at the woods. Dad parked the car against the trees and I slowly got out of the car. It was already getting dark. We all settled down and put our tents up.

Mom and Dad were going to bed. I started to fall asleep when through my tent, I could make out a human shadow. I thought it was just Mom or Dad. Suddenly, the shadow started unzipping my tent door. I was terrified.

I slowly went to the edge of my tent, scared to death. The door of the tent opened and I was never seen again...

Sara Curillova (10)
Cumnor CE Primary School, Cumnor

Secret Mission

I sprinted out with the cookies in my hand and said to my mom, "Bye!"
I slammed the door.
My best friend was waiting for me. We sprinted to the woods. We ate the cookies with joy.
"Yum!" we said.
Then we heard *hiss! Hiss!* It was a black mamba snake.
My friend said, "I know that was a black mamba because it's the fastest snake in the world."
We were scared for our lives. We ran back to our houses and laid in our cosy beds.

Harrison Daci
Cumnor CE Primary School, Cumnor

Murder Among The Trees

There must be a way out. The boy stood at the giant rose-red mushrooms and the towering trees around him. As twilight faded into night, he saw a note that was pinned to a tree with a knife. The note was bloodstained. It said that he was next... He knew he was going to be killed. Then he heard it... A laugh that shattered through the forest. He ran and ran. He saw a knife zoom past him. The killer had thrown the knife. The boy nearly made it out but he failed to...

Benjamin Robinson (11)

Cumnor CE Primary School, Cumnor

The Feisty Pair Of Pants

"Tom!" his mum yelled. "Just go somewhere, anywhere!"

Equally fed up, Tom trudged to the woods.

Having walked miles, he eventually found a pair of plain pants. Curiously, he put them on. To his surprise, the pants objected.

"Oi! Ouch!" yelled Tom. "You bit my bum and have given me an almighty wedgie!"

The pants lifted a terrified Tom up into the air.

"Save me!" he pleaded.

They flew over the woods and hovered over his street, where the pants abruptly and tipped him out.

Landing on a drainpipe, Tom exclaimed, "Well, this is uncomfortable!"

And there he stayed.

Theo Haines (10)
Daneshill School, Hook

Owlbert And Owlweene

Feather bombs dropped as two owls gazed into each other's eyes.

"I'll always remember you, Owlweene," whispered Owlbert in his dark voice.

Owlweene spoke softly, "It can't end like this, my darling Owlbert."

The two owls tried desperately to escape their morbid fate and stay together.

The bird war between their families raged on. Owlbert convinced Owlweene to sneak away with him. With great daring, they snuck past the terrifying Wood Dragons, who guarded the forest. One snorted and stirred. The owls froze in cold fear. Luckily, the dragon had not awoken. The owl lovers escaped and lived together happily.

Elouisa Preston-Sparrow (10)

Daneshill School, Hook

The Enigmatic Washing Line

Once, there was a mysterious washing line that could teleport anywhere. All one had to do was select a country, wear the clothes provided and enjoy the exhilaration of teleportation.

Dwarf Dreamy and Elf Twinkle dreamt of travelling somewhere warm. They selected a destination and marvelled as the remarkable washing line began rotating quicker than the speed of light.

Bang! The machine had faltered. They arrived at their dream location, only it wasn't somewhere hot. Howls of angry wind echoed sorrowfully. The putrid trees reeked and bugs scarpered across them. This wasn't Bliss Island, it was the deadly Peril Forest!

Saffi Raj (10)

Daneshill School, Hook

The Agonising Ailment

A tree named Kosmont was listening to the chirrup of the robins amidst the trees. Unexpectedly, he felt a searing pain ascending up his roots. Determined to know what was happening, he sent a badger, named Rocky, to investigate. Tunnelling deep underground, Rocky soon hit solid floor. Before he had time to react, a voice screeched, "Have you come to deprive me of my wand?" Rocky had no influence, however, a wand soared through the ravine.

"Nooo!" the creature howled in frustration, as a cauldron stopped bubbling.

Rocky dashed back to Kosmont, thrilled to have saved him from eternal suffering.

Milo Ramage (9)
Daneshill School, Hook

Into The Magical World

In the distance, I saw ancient steel gates spilt with moss and ivy. Heart-shaped leaves dangled lazily on their stalks. Creaking open, the gate allowed me to slowly trudge in before clanging shut behind me.

Fearing there was no escape, my thoughts were shattered when two tiny unicorns galloped towards me.

"Poachers took Mother," one spluttered.

Somehow, I understood them. Mounting one unicorn's back, we flew over the forest, spotting their mother trapped in a cruel cage.

Dismounting, I sprinted over and pulled at the cage to free her. To my surprise, it worked. Had this world turned me magical?

Chloe Guthrie (9)

Daneshill School, Hook

The Mysterious Light

In the distance, I spotted an archaic cottage with inexplicable purple and yellow beams shining from it. Venturing inside, I realised that the light wasn't from there.

Outside, I searched everywhere until finally discovering the answer. Behind the quaint cottage stood an eerie shed. Its dilapidated door was hanging off its hinges. I cautiously stepped inside where I discovered a deep, cavernous hole.

At the bottom, there were two dazzling fairies who had been captured by a nefarious witch. Daringly, I set them free.

To show their gratitude, they invited me to their exquisite home in the enchanted forest.

Roselie du Bruyn (10)

Daneshill School, Hook

Forest Friends

Once upon a time, there was a chocolate brownie called CB. He was the kindest creature in the forest and a guardian of some luxurious, sparkling treasure. Everyone in the forest often talked about this precious treasure.

A strange shadow strolled into the forest and camped there overnight.

The next day, the mysterious figure knocked on CB's door. It said, "I'm Ice Cream and I'm here for your treasure!"

CB was outraged and battled Ice Cream to protect the treasure.

The battle waged on for several hours. Eventually, a tired CB was victorious. The summer sun had melted Ice Cream.

Riley Moncrieff (10)
Daneshill School, Hook

The Rose Of Spirit!

Diamonds and rubies dangled from the bushes and pixies clung onto trees. Phelina sat on her throne, high on the hill. What a gorgeous phoenix she was! A terrible illness spread through the pixie population. There was only one cure, Phelina's rose, the most spirited rose ever discovered.
With great speed, she placed the rose in the enchanted lake. the crystal-clear water glowed. All the pixies clung tightly to the trees. Soon, they began whispering quietly, then chattered, then giggled, not knowing what had just happened. Phelina felt content with what she had achieved. The wood was once again happy!

Poppy Molloy (10)
Daneshill School, Hook

Spirits

Heavenly white and gold spirits used to roam the magical forest. Tranquillity was broken when humans started cutting down trees. This made the spirits furious, turning them evil. Deep purple spirits now roam the forest, pent up with rage. Many humans have been victim to these spirits, viciously swallowed into the undergrowth, never to be seen again. Something had to be done.

Nature began repairing itself as the Water Moons calmed the evil spirits. Well-meaning humans began planting more trees, replacing those that had been chopped down.

Colourful, calm spirits now fly around the forest sky, happy once more.

Emily David (10)
Daneshill School, Hook

A House At Halloween

It was Halloween. To celebrate, I invited my friends to our hangout. We walked through the winding paths of Hazel Wood until we reached our destination. Astonishingly, our hangout had vanished! In its place was a creepy mansion that stood huge and menacing before us.

Charlie opened the door and walked inside. Izzy and I followed closely. It was the wrong decision. All the blinds fell down on their own accord and the windows and doors locked.

"We're prisoners," Izzy whispered.

My worst nightmare had come true. Desperately, we yelled for help. nobody came. It was the end for us...

Miriam Kimber (10)

Daneshill School, Hook

The Evil Game

Once upon a time, on a bright morning, the gnome tribes rested. One gnome, called Timmy, heard a weird noise. It sounded like "Umbachaka!"
Then a threatening voice commanded Timmy.
"Turn evil and destroy all your tribe. Kill them all. Youngest to oldest. If you can do that, then you will rule the world!"
The evil voice belonged to Jeff, the meanest, nastiest gnome in the whole wood. When Timmy refused his orders, an angry Jeff kidnapped him.
"I can force you to do what I want," Jeff hissed. Luckily, Timmy managed to escape. Jeff continued plotting alone.

Ted Brownfield (9)
Daneshill School, Hook

The Two Book Trees

Once upon a time, there lived three elves, James, John and Ellie.

One day, Ellie went to the woods to pick some scrumptious berries. Suddenly, a gremlin came out of the earth and bit her on the leg.

Hearing Ellie's cries, James ran to help and placed her in front of the healing oak tree. Their nightmare didn't end there.

John sprinted towards them, shouting, "Wolves coming, run!"

Too late. Hungry wolves leapt from the shadows and circled them, snarling. They edged back towards the oak tree. The powerful tree calmed the wolves and the three elves made their escape.

James Mason (9)
Daneshill School, Hook

War In The Woods

Once upon a time, there was a small village in the middle of ancient woods. In the village, lived powerful gnomes and dwarves.
One day, King Dwarf discovered a magical ring that corrupted him, turning him greedy and selfish. He started a war between the dwarves and the gnomes, making them bitter enemies.
King Gnome realised there was something wrong. King Dwarf was acting peculiar and wasn't himself. In the morning, King Gnome secretly snuck into King Dwarf's room and destroyed the ring. With the evil curse broken, King Dwarf apologised and from then on, they all lived in peace.

Charlie Downs (10)

Daneshill School, Hook

The Forest's Secret

Ella almost disappeared from view as Patricia chased after her, unfortunately falling over the root of an oak tree. Looking up from the ground, she noticed the sun's glint highlighting a mysterious, shiny key.

Ella joined Patricia and helped her up. They were amazed to see that there was a keyhole in the tree! Patricia tried the key and was shocked to find that it fitted perfectly.

Suddenly, the trees around them exploded, spraying fairy dust all over them. As they looked around, they saw an army of leaves attacking innocent woodland animals. Their quest was clear... protect the woods.

Leela Chauhan (10)
Daneshill School, Hook

No Ordinary Dragon

Once upon a time, there was an extraordinary dragon called Blaze, who lived alone in a remote rainforest. Unlike normal dragons, Blaze was small and flabby, wobbling like jelly when he moved. One day, Blaze strolled through the forest where he discovered a deep, dark cave. He peered inside and was stunned to see a cluster of dazzling fairies. He cautiously entered but his pot belly got entangled in a spiderweb, causing him to scream. Hearing the noise, the petrified fairies scattered away.

Blaze apologised and begged the fairies to cure his loneliness. This they did and a friendship grew.

Millie Swarbrick (9)
Daneshill School, Hook

The Fairy Switch

In a magical wood, there lived two types of enchanted fairies. The summer fairies lived in one half of the vast wood, in eternal sunshine, while the winter fairies lived in the other half full of glossy snow.

One extraordinary day, a spiteful witch lured the summer fairies into the crisp snow and the winter fairies into the amber warmth. At first, the winter fairies had difficulty flying as they were blisteringly hot. The summer fairies were as cold as the witch's heart.

Over time, the fairies adapted to their new environments, but life was never quite the same again.

Megan Harrison (9)

Daneshill School, Hook

The Terrifying Troll

Once upon a time in a dark, gloomy forest, there was a little mushroom fairy known as Blossom, and her adorable poodle, Fluffy.

Their tranquillity was shattered by a noise. They knew they were not alone. Out came the terrifying troll! The protective Fluffy barked at him loudly. Blossom tried to run, but it was too late. The troll captured her and took her away.

Fluffy was devastated. He united all the woodland creatures to help him save Blossom.

They marched to the troll's lair, knocked him out by firing magical acorns at him and rescued poor Blossom safely.

Kate Hursey (9)
Daneshill School, Hook

Doughnut Head

Once upon a time, there was a little girl called Willow. She decided to go to her favourite place, the mysterious dark woods, at the edge of the village.

Skipping along the path, she went through the gate. Suddenly, she felt weird and tingly in her brain. It was almost as if her head was a strange, different shape.

She returned home but her parents didn't recognise her at all. She looked in the mirror and screamed. The reflection staring back at her was a huge, sticky, colourful doughnut with saucer eyes and sprinkle eyelashes.

Nothing was the same again...

Lola Franklin Adams (10)

Daneshill School, Hook

The Myth That Came True

Once, there was a honey badger called Sweets and an elk called Midget. They decided to go on a walk through the wood, known as Death Valley. Although they were wary of the myth about a naked ostrich that kidnapped anything that came in its direction, they decided to go anyway.

At first, it seemed normal but the further they went, the creepier it got. Suddenly, Midget felt Sweets fly off his back. He turned to find himself facing the kidnapping naked ostrich.

In a heroic gesture, Midget rammed the naked ostrich with all his strength and saved petrified Sweets.

Sammy Langly-Smith (9)
Daneshill School, Hook

Stumpy

Two proud gecko parents had the joy of having three babies. Unfortunately, one, named Stumpy, was born missing his two back legs.
Heartbreakingly, his parents rejected him, sending him tumbling out of the warm family nest.
He sadly fell down the tree, bumped and bruised. Frightened, Stumpy tried hard to climb up and down the huge leaves. Danger attacked in the form of a hungry swooping bird who deftly grabbed Stumpy and flew him to her nest.
Just in time, Stumpy slipped out of her beak and jumped onto a branch. There, a kind chameleon looked after Stumpy forever.

Rupert Fitzgerald (10)
Daneshill School, Hook

The Rescue

I arrived at the secret meeting place with the others. It was midnight and there were loud monster howls marking our Queen's disappearance. It was hard to know what happened. Because of their war against the unknown, it ended in the monsters kidnapping our Queen.

Finally, we hatched a plan. We agreed to wear masks to not be noticed. We found the Queen's location at the headquarters and went through the window. the monster's base was in the middle of the woods. Trees were crying in pain, due to being chopped down. The Queen climbed out and was rescued.

Stan Britz (10)

Daneshill School, Hook

The Elements

I arrived at the secret meeting place and entered the Elements room. I spotted the guard dragon asleep, which was strange because only powerful sorcerers could put guard dragons to sleep with fire dust. Realising this, I hid behind a pillar, scared for my life. When I saw Shadow, who I'd arranged to meet, I was so relieved.

She said darkly, "You'd never have guessed it was me."

Cold dread filled my body. She picked up the water stone which immediately turned black. There would be no water in the wood now and there was nothing I could do...

Mirabelle Selby (9)
Daneshill School, Hook

My Death

My father, a sagacious werewolf, was forced to fight for our lives. He left me alone and heartbroken to protect me.

One cruel morning, I was anxious when I realised I was out of food. I only had one choice, I had to race to the woods to forage for food.

Dashing through the bushes, I could smell the familiar scent of fresh rabbit. Suddenly, The Nothing appeared out of nowhere. He strangled me and I felt myself plummeting to the cold, hard ground. My eyes closed slowly as I said goodbye to my life.

Now I'm with my father.

Lois Hughes (10)

Daneshill School, Hook

The Fairy's Granted

Once, there was a fairy strolling through the woods when she spotted a little girl named Amy, running at top speed, not looking where she was going. Just then, the fairy, who was called Dixie, flew up to Amy, fluttering her wings delicately as she did so. The girl looked in amazement as Dixie took her hand and led her through a giant barrier.

There, a tall man stood with a crown on his head. Amy told them both about what happened and expressed her desire to be a fairy, just like them. Eventually, her delightful wish came true.

Josephine Oliphant (10)
Daneshill School, Hook

Losing Barney

I'd been running for what seemed like days but it'd been minutes. I was lost in the forest and completely soaked. My mind was racing! His pained face still tormented me. He was gone. It should have been me. My mood was dark, like the forest. Thinking back to the moment that changed my life, sent shivers down my spine.

We'd been playing with matches when Barney had begged to strike one. Encouraging him was a mistake. The forest ignited in flames, taking Barney in its hot grip. How could I ever explain my part in this?

Lenny Smith (9)
Daneshill School, Hook

The Green War

I was walking when I heard rustling in the bushes. It was getting dark so I just ignored it. In the woods in front of me, I saw a light.

All of a sudden, a goblin appeared from the bushes and threw a sharp, wooden spear at me. I tried to duck. From the light, came the White Dragon covered in frost. The dragon breathed icicles out of his nostrils, which froze the spear that was heading towards me like lightning. The goblin was also frozen. Both shattered into ice dust.

I would forever be grateful to the White Dragon.

Jasper Crowther (10)
Daneshill School, Hook

The Pack

In a hidden forest, I came across three werewolves who needed my help to cure their brother. We raced through the night by the light of the full moon until we reached an oak tree.

At the little door, I turned the handle. A startling sight met our eyes. There, in the gloom, was a golden tree! One werewolf dug up a root.

Once in his jaws, he bolted back to the dying boy and wiped the root juice on his face. Suddenly, he was transformed back into a werewolf. Joining the pack, he howled delightedly and they were gone.

Olive Bailey (10)
Daneshill School, Hook

Hero

My heart was pounding. I was dashing and darting through the towering trees, jumping over the broken branches. I looked back. They were gaining on me. I was so close to home, just one more stretch.

Scrambling to my den, I quickly, deftly covered the entrance, just before they saw me. I collapsed to the floor in relief. Evil voices bellowed, "We will find you and you will pay!"

I whimpered as I retreated to the back of my den. There was so much work to do. I absolutely had to protect the animals...

Emma Wheeler (10)

Daneshill School, Hook

An Unusual Hunt

Jack, a boy aged thirteen, got his bow and went into the woods with his dog.

As he got deeper, he heard weird noises. Then he heard a deep voice telling him to beware of the woodland ghost.

A little while later, he saw the shadow, made of dark mist, floating around. Then the ghost attacked Jack and his dog. Before anyone was hurt, a falcon flew in and scared away the woodland ghost.

Then it spoke to Jack and his dog about some edible mushrooms near where they were. Jack picked them and went home.

John Love (10)
Daneshill School, Hook

The Battle Of The Demons

There was a forest and it was dark. In that forest were ninja snails fighting each other. Not far from there, some frogs, not ordinary frogs, were performing a ritual.

The snails had been taken over by a demon snaked and turned into slave snails.

The frogs had been killed by a demon. The demon's name was Joew. The demon frog was heading for the demon snake and it was a fight to the death.

It lasted for a decade... Just kidding, it only lasted five minutes and it ended the snails' fight.

Henry Francis (10)

Daneshill School, Hook

Infiltrated

This was a disaster. I was late for the secret meeting. I rushed down the road with my keycard. I sprinted into the old, worn house and ripped off a plank from the floor which led into a slide-like pipe. I dived into it. *Whoosh!* I was in a futuristic, bright white room. I swiped the card and the door opened...

We had been infiltrated. All the furniture was sprawled across the floor in pieces. I was flabbergasted. Desperately, I searched for it in the never-ending pile of debris. The precious last ever KitKat had been taken.

"Thief!" I screamed.

Rahul Mackinlay (10)

Eveline Day School, Tooting

A Wander In The Woods

The dense woods were alive with sound; creaking laughter from the swaying trees, the high chatter of birds. The raindrops sang through the air before smashing into the ground with a satisfying hiss. But I wasn't here for that. The moon shone a milky lustre down on the world, bathing it in white.
As I grew nearer, clay pots filled with yellow flames danced in the crisp night air. Then the ground turned from spongy moss to a well-trodden path. I glanced around. I could see many bright eyes watching me through the mat of twisted, twining vegetation...

Stanley Taylor (11)
Eveline Day School, Tooting

The Mirror

In the distance, I saw my reflection staring back at me. But I wasn't the same. I was different. I looked around but no one was there. The woods were completely silent. The only noises were the animals making sounds.

I stood still and looked at the mirror again. A crazy idea sprang into my mind. I stepped into the mirror...

A new world opened up and I looked just like the other person in the mirror. Everything was so different. No wonder the mirror looked strange. I thought, *what adventures are waiting for me now...?*

Maria Kostyleva (9)

Eveline Day School, Tooting

My Walk Last Night

It was getting dark. I felt as if I had arthritic fingers as it was so cold. My tummy was swirling around in circles and I was lost. Where was I? How do I get home?

I tiptoed forward as quiet as a mouse, hoping I would find my way out of the forest... Would I? The vegetation was dense and the shadows were large. As night started to approach, I started to get tired. Someone shouted my name.

"Where are you?" they shouted.

I looked around. My friend, Charlotte, popped out from behind a tree. They'd found me.

Lili Marley (9)
Eveline Day School, Tooting

A Whole New World

It was getting dark. I was in the middle of a dense and gloomy forest. There were no people at all, just pure darkness. I crept through the forest to get some wood. In no time at all, I'd built a shelter. I went to get more wood for the fire.

I stumbled into a magical portal. There I was, in a whole new world. I admired all the blossom trees. Then I found a shimmering castle. Suddenly, I was trapped like a bird in a cage. This castle of great riches was just a horrid illusion...

Leo Thomas Brannan (9)
Eveline Day School, Tooting

The Wizard And The Elf

It was getting dark and lifeless. The wizard and elf were marching towards the secret meeting place in the mysterious, unexplored forest. Anxiously, he was hoping that the fairy and the unicorn had made up their minds to go through the enchanted red wall with him to gain supreme magic. Unfortunately, none of them were ready to take the risk.

Excited at the sight of the eerie wall, he offered to share with them his magical powers. Eventually, they agreed and jumped across the mystical wall. However, to their surprise, they fell into a gloomy, ghostly cave with no escape...

Fatimah Khan (8)
GEMS Founders School - Al Mizah, Dubai

Sam And The Dungeon

One day, Sam woke up and went to his attic. He found a lever and pulled it. It took him to a creepy forest at night.

He started looking around and heard a roar. He felt terrified. He found a tent and survived there for a couple of days.

It started to feel like he was being watched. He looked around the woods and found a dead horse. He said, "Who's killing these animals?"

He found a pathway and a stone wall. It was a dungeon.

"Argh!" he said...

Yousef Nagi (8)
GEMS Founders School - Al Mizah, Dubai

The Poor Cat

One day, my brother and I wanted a kitten, so we persuaded our parents to get one.

At last, we found the perfect female kitten from Uptown Mirdif. After welcoming it, it was shy but got used to us.

Later, the cat started being as active as a tiger but soon it got diarrhoea and became lazy.

It was sick, so we took it to the vets until it was healthy. We missed it a lot and went to see it every day.

Sadly, the cat died...

Ali Hamza Hasan Sadiq (8)

GEMS Founders School - Al Mizah, Dubai

The Mystery...

'Twas dark and Ryan ran, he saw the woods and hid. From what? Suddenly, he saw a huge place with an Among Us tower. Ryan went in, he saw a portal and went in. He was in the *airship!* He saw Innersloth, he said, "You are in danger. You need my help."
Suddenly, Novisor came and they ran for their lives...

Rayaan Rauf (9)
Lady Royd Primary, Bradford

The Girl Who Was Sploshed

Once upon a time, lived a girl called Shelly. she wanted to prank her brother, Tom, by splashing water on his head, but she splashed it on herself! She was sad and went to the forest.

She fell into a hole and found a trophy. She decided she would keep it. She started crying and she did for four hours.

Her mum and dad started to worry. They put up posters but there was still no sign of Shelly. Her brother, Tom, was happy but then Shelly got home safely.

Anu Oyetade (8)

Lark Hill Community Primary School, Salford

Lilly And The Creepy Forest!

Once upon a time, there was a secret door and a girl called Lilly. She was the one that'd found the door. She went inside and found some treasure. "This is a weird place," said Lilly.

She started to hear noises behind her. She was shocked when she saw a big green goblin looking at her eyes! She thought that her eyes had powers. Then guess what? She did have powers. She killed the goblin with just a blink. She was surprised she could shoot lasers.

She ran through the door, back to safety.

Harry Davies (9)
Leighswood School, Aldridge

A Strange Noise

In the distance, I saw a huge tree that was about to fall on the floor. It had apples on it. There was a massive puddle where it was going to land.
All of a sudden, I could hear a strange noise in the distance. I turned around and could hear the noise again. Then it came closer and closer. I looked behind me. I saw a fox. It was really friendly. It came up to me. It was starting to get cold so we went to find sticks to make fire. It blazed...

Macie Williams (9)
Leighswood School, Aldridge

Little Red Riding Hood

One day, there was a hungry wolf. He saw a girl called Little Red Riding Hood. He asked the girl where she lived and snuck into her house. He hid inside her wardrobe full of clothes.

Little Red Riding Hood, once she'd visited her nana's with a bunch of flowers, merrily skipped back to her beloved home. She walked in through the front door and then to her bedroom, where she got the shock of her life! The wolf jumped out of nowhere and killed her.

Luckily, Little Red Riding Hood awoke and found it was all a dream.

Hannah Bradley (9)
Lenham Primary School, Lenham

The Lost Camper

One day, Chris' friends told him to head into the woods. He was to have no resources, just a tent. Ten hours later, he was ready to go. Chris hated being on slow trains but he soon made it to the location.

Chris quickly set up his tent and fell asleep. He was not alone... A creepy, dark figure with blood-red eyes stood over him.

In the morning, Chris prepared breakfast and went walking until dark. Mysteriously, he was guided somewhere unknown. There was no trace of Chris. Was he back, the flesh-rotting, red-eyed stealer?

Oliver Smith (11)
Martin Wilson School, Castlefields

The Light That Night

As he walked through the woods, he saw a light in the distance. As he walked closer to the source of the light he heard a light high-pitched humming sound. The humming got louder and louder as he got closer and closer. Soon, before he knew it, he was in front of the light source, the light was blinding. He touched it. There was a flash of light, the light was gone and so was he.

A light appeared and so did the boy, the light disappeared but this time the boy was left alone.

Lucie Vis (11)
Newtonmore Primary School, Newtonmore

Enchantia

"A long time ago, in the faraway kingdom of Enchantia, lived two sisters, Crystal and Diamond. They lived a happy life until one night, Diamond went over to her grandfather's statue and started to say a spell to lure the spirits. She wanted all of the power and wanted to start an era of dark magic. Crystal saw what was happening so she climbed up the statue, but the spirits wrapped around her and started to absorb her life. Years later Crystal was getting healed but the spirits didn't go."
A howl of wind came and Amber's fire went out...

Georgia Bibin (11)
Russells Hall Primary School, Russells Hall Estate

Ollie's Birthday Celebration Ruined

There once lived a dog named Ollie that lived in Dudley. Ollie had black velvet fur with a nice cute cuddly face.

There was a massive celebration going on today, Ollie's birthday! There were loads of colourful balloons, a big yummy cake and loads of animal friends, Bob the elephant and Izzy the dog. Oh no, Dingo just kidnapped Izzy... he left a note saying 'Revenge!' That's when Ollie and Bob decided to go after Dingo to end all the drama. Dingo was caught and arrested and Izzy was bought to safety and they all lived happily ever after.

Josh Bullock (11)

Russells Hall Primary School, Russells Hall Estate

The Mystery Of The Forest

Wandering in the woods is beautiful. You meet many animals. My favourite animal is the deer. Some time ago, when I was on a walk through the forest, I saw a beautiful deer. He had great antlers and was enormous. He was standing on the hill staring at the setting sun. I stood motionless for a while because I was afraid the deer would attack me. He didn't. He stood proudly with large antlers raised high. I left him alone, slowly backing away so as not to scare him. When I got home I told my brother about my adventure.

Victoria Jednorog (10)

Russells Hall Primary School, Russells Hall Estate

Game Woods

Three boys had wandered into a mysterious forest, Ron, Jack and Jay, they had no idea what they'd walked into. First, they were surrounded by animals. Jack was taken by a moose and was dropped in a 20-foot hole and Jay was taken by an owl, but Ron ran after Jack, he distracted the moose and got Jack out and they ran to get Jay who was in a maze, but when they got to the maze there was a button that lit up the way out. When Jay got out he saw a portal saying 'next level'...

Mckenzie Garland (11)

Russells Hall Primary School, Russells Hall Estate

Terror In The Woods...

The wind whistled through the ancient trees as I wandered deeper into the woods. It felt too quiet and eerie and I knew I needed to escape this horrifying feeling. In the corner of my eye, I could sense eyes on me. My heart pounded like an animal trying to escape my chest. As panic stirred, I ran like a cheetah after its prey.

That's when I had the feeling of being chased... I stumbled across the luminous stream and glanced over my shoulder at a ferocious creature. I stumbled back over the misshapen rocks, falling to the ground...

Kyle Phillips (9)

Short Heath Junior School, Willenhall

The Mystery

It had been weeks, my friends and I were searching the dark abandoned mansion for clues. "Have you found anything?" I asked impatiently.

"No," replied Jimmy.

Crash! Something happened in the kitchen. Raymond. He went missing. "What happened?" questioned Lily. We explained what happened to Raymond and I soon realised Rebecca was also missing.

A few days later, Lily vanished too. I was struck with fear. When we looked in the old, decaying basement, something brushed past me along with Jimmy receding. Who could it be? Rebecca, she's betrayed me! "Help!" It was the end!

Munachim Okoliocha (10)
St Aidan's Catholic Primary Academy, Ilford

The Voice Inside My Head

I keep hearing voices; my ears ringing. Breathing heavily, my eyes flicker to a close. I picture a girl speaking to nobody and hear my name being called. "Evie! Evie!" It's no one.
I'm hallucinating.
My mind suddenly goes blank.
All I can hear is someone saying, "There is no *voice*, Evie. It's just you." Then they repeat themselves again and again.

5 months later...
Then I realise something about everything, except the girl; it's just me...
I'm fine now, right?
No, there's something about that girl, she's in my nightmares...

Idah Milla Mkandawire (10)
St Aidan's Catholic Primary Academy, Ilford

A Wander In The Woods

I trudged through the autumn leaves; sparkling crystals glittered in the twinkling sky. There it was... a rundown shack; George's home. The door was ajar, the house seemed vacant - no sound. I listened again - no sound. Dashing in, unthinking, my hands ached for gold. Scouring every place, I was about to leave when I discovered grains of sand scattered evenly on the floorboards. Where could this have come from? I peered under... "A sack of guineas!" I said foolishly.

Rushing out, I forgot the quarry mine and plunged into it. I checked in the sack. Bricks. Rocks exploded... *Boom!*

Ilham Quddus (10)

St Aidan's Catholic Primary Academy, Ilford

The Manhunt

The leaves rustled behind me as the wind brushed against my face. If I stopped, they were sure to catch me. A billion thoughts rushed through my head as I tried to do something spectacularly spontaneous. *Snap!* The branch I was standing on fell into a bush!
I saw them suspiciously fading away into the distance. I rushed over toward the portal's remains and scattered around cautiously paranoid. When I found the last piece of portal I didn't think twice about summoning it immediately. During my travels to the underworld, I realised I wasn't the only one who'd disappeared...

Luke McMorrow (11)
St Aidan's Catholic Primary Academy, Ilford

Mimic

I clutched Emiyada's missing poster whilst the wind wailed north. I had to hurry, the rush of the air was getting faster with each second.

A hallway, plain white. I expected something more 'antiquated'. As the lights blinked, a smidgeon of blood appeared, forming a trail. Interesting...

It stopped at a dead end. Singing could be heard miles away. It got louder and louder, meaning 'she' was close... *Crack! Bash!*

The strand of agony, a thorny stem of a rose. She peered down at me. She wasn't Emiyada. So, who was she? Why was she here? What was she?

Michelle Okena (10)

St Aidan's Catholic Primary Academy, Ilford

The Eye

Crack! I escaped. Three dreadful years and I was finally able to see. I'd created a way to see things differently with the third eye. Things we'd never imagined...

Police sirens going crazy, racing through filthy bushes. What could I do? *Crunch!* Everything went silent... Running fast, I was there: the headquarters. A dangerous place full of wires and the unknown...

Hacking through high-tech computers, trying to show the blind... it worked! Shame I couldn't stay. I was moving to a new planet. It was stunning. They wouldn't arrest me there!

Liyana Miah (11)

St Aidan's Catholic Primary Academy, Ilford

An Unusual Encounter

It was approaching. I had no time. I was lost and didn't know what it was. It was advancing, however, I couldn't help but admire the scenery: birds, trees, mushrooms - it was beautiful. Suddenly, I heard a rustle - then footsteps. I ran. I was sprinting like a cheetah, so fast I had no idea where I was heading, thinking I would get away. But then the tables turned! I fell, slipping, rolling and gashing my thigh. There was no escape - I was done for. It came but I realised that I was running from a *Raid Shadow Legends* advertisement. *Wow*!

Aydin Rahman (11)
St Aidan's Catholic Primary Academy, Ilford

Discovering My Superpowers

In the distance, Jack and I saw a magnificent forest. Little did we know it wasn't a normal type of forest. Then... *boom!* We were extremely confused. I started to investigate... Every step towards the sound sent a tingly feeling up my spine. Then I heard laughing, singing, crunching. The trees started to collapse, massive spiders climbed all over me. I heard Jack pull out a gun and shoot at me. I panicked! It started happening in slow motion, but I was so scared. I didn't even notice my hand jump in front of the bullet and... well... catch it!

Dylan Velenia-Magallona (10)
St Aidan's Catholic Primary Academy, Ilford

A Wander In The Woods

Snap! Snap! I've found it! The mysterious wooden door. I wondered why it was boarded up. I ripped off the planks and opened the door. It was purple inside and there was a breeze. I stepped inside. *Whoosh!* I started spinning. My head was banging and my stomach was churning.

All of a sudden, something started chasing me. It had a magical object in its hand. Then it started shooting at me with it.

"Ouch!" I cried.

Something hard hit me. I fell to the ground and the creature began to approach me...

Cristiano Fernandes (11)

St Aidan's Catholic Primary Academy, Ilford

The Fancy Dream

While I was walking in the woods, in the distance, I saw a tree glowing. It seemed like a door. I opened it. What a surprise!
I was in another world. *Whoosh!* There were glowing mushrooms, stars dancing and a glowing green dog. There were gigantic frogs flying in the sky. Panic zipped through me and I ran as far as I could. I couldn't reach the door.
After some time, I was calm. I met the green dog. His name was Bobbly. We had fun together. Bobbly's house was glowing.
I had the fanciest dream ever!

Divya Ashna Beekawoo (11)
St Aidan's Catholic Primary Academy, Ilford

The Forest Nightmare

"Mayday, mayday, we're going down!"
"Flight 2703, do you copy?"
It was the 9th January, 2009. We were nearing Brazil airport and I was excited to see the Brazillian rainforest, unaware it would soon be my greatest nightmare.
At 3,000ft I ran out of fuel and was plummeting towards the surface, 50ft per second. I had to think fast. In a matter of a minute, I would collide with the centre of the Earth.
My heart was racing, my hands were trembling, I didn't want to die...

Arun Jindal (11)

St Aidan's Catholic Primary Academy, Ilford

Dead End

My chance had begun. In the distance, a castle, tall and arched. I wasn't safe but it was time. I walked towards it knowing it was the only thing I could do. Crunching through leaves, breaking twigs along the way. I made it but was locked out. I had no time. I heard a noise. The sound of big, heavy footsteps getting louder. I hid behind a tree, frightened of what was to come. I couldn't believe I wasn't alone after all this time.
They opened the door and I sneakily followed behind...

Tyra Chikandira (11)
St Aidan's Catholic Primary Academy, Ilford

Portal

One gloomy night, a flash of light came from Green Highwood. A flicker of fire came over the sky. Some teens saw the portal.

"Holy moly! What is that?" they all shouted.

"Let's go back..." whispered one of them.

Suddenly, they tripped over a vine. All of a sudden, *zap!* They were gone...

Twenty years later...

The world was running low on metals. The idea was to go to other dimensions to steal their metals. Suddenly, the same bright blue portal appeared at Green Highwood. A man stepped forward.

"It's our only hope," he sighed and stepped in. *Zap!*

Theo Melchor Cahilig (8)

St Augustine's Catholic Primary School, Leeds

The People In Black

It was getting dark, but Brad was still awake. He was going to tell his parents something but they weren't downstairs. He went outside and found himself in a forest.

After years, he came upon a day where it was very foggy. Lost, he stumbled upon a stick. Thankfully, he landed on a pile of leaves. He was suspicious as to why the pile of leaves was there. He looked around and found a small door. He heard a yell. People started chasing him. *Bang!*

When he regained consciousness, he realised that the people chasing him were his missing parents.

Sachi Trinidad Go (8)
St Augustine's Catholic Primary School, Leeds

The Dangerous Werewolf

One day, a boy and his friends went on a school trip to the forest.

When it was night-time a dangerous werewolf took the teachers somewhere.

The next night, the children heard weird noises. Suddenly, they saw a werewolf and it started chasing them. The werewolf caught one of them but couldn't catch the others.

In the morning, they tried to find their teachers.

A few hours later, they found their teachers. But then they saw the werewolf. A dragon then blocked the entrance to the teachers. It knelt down and after they were all free.

Mujtaba Alizadah (8)

St Augustine's Catholic Primary School, Leeds

The Night In The Wood

I heard a noise behind me. I looked. It was white with black eyes.

"There's no such thing as ghosts!"

My campmates had vanished into the gloomy forest. I ran to my phone and called my teacher but there was no signal.

The police came to the woods and I asked them to give me a ride. I told them what happened. Luckily, they believed me.

Scientists had invented a machine to catch ghosts. The police used it and found all my friends.

When the police came back they told everyone to keep the machine a secret...

Rahmel Maynard (8)
St Augustine's Catholic Primary School, Leeds

A Wander In The Woods

Once upon a time, there was a boy named Aaron.
He lived in a wooden shack by the woods.
One day, Aaron wanted to go into the mystical
wood because he heard a strange voice coming
from there.
It said, "Come to me, Aaron."
Aaron went into the dark and mystical woods. He
fell through a portal and landed on a dragon.
Suddenly, the dragon began to talk to him.
"Oh, hey! Where did you come from?"
Aaron replied, "A... portal!"
Aaron looked around and wanted to stay there.

Anna Więckiewicz (8)

St Augustine's Catholic Primary School, Leeds

The Mysterious Forest

It was getting dark. A forest of magical mystery awaited. Trees waved in the breeze, flowers danced in the mist.

I heard something in the distance. Behind me was a gloomy cave. I went inside and saw loads of crystals and diamonds.

I saw a lady. She said she'd put a curse on the forest and that the tree of the curse was five hours away from the forest.

I decided to find it. I finally found it. I invited my friend to help me destroy it. We tried until we finally did it. The forest was safe.

Maria Braganza (8)

St Augustine's Catholic Primary School, Leeds

The Kidnapper Ghost

It was getting dark and when I woke up, all I could remember was walking from school to home. I was trapped in a secret base.

I searched for my phone so that I could call for help. Suddenly, I heard a creaking noise. A door opened. Then out came a zombie. I got up and started to run. *Crash!* I bumped into a wall. I touched slowly around the wall and I felt a switch. I flicked it on. There stood all my friends dressed in spooky Halloween costumes. It was my friends' Halloween trick!

Nikitha Chelladurai (8)

St Augustine's Catholic Primary School, Leeds

The Spy Girl Who Saved The Day

One day, there was a girl called Lizza.

One night, she had a dream. In the dream, she was in the dark. She was walking. Soon, she saw a mysterious gate. She got scared but she opened the gate.

Suddenly, a bad group came, called the RHS. They were talking about how they would trap a girl called Rebecca. Lizza was spying on them.

She quietly sneaked into their lair and saved Rebecca's family and Rebecca...

Isabella Obiri Yeboah (9)

St Augustine's Catholic Primary School, Leeds

The Mist

Once upon a time, there was a boy called Justin. He was walking with his friends in the woods. They came upon a campfire. It was still lit, so it couldn't have been there for long. There was a tent and a mist trail that led into a dark cave. It looked scary and went on for a bit.

After a long walk through the cave, they came to two paths. Two boys went left and two went right. The boys that went right heard screams from the other boys. The screaming boys came running back, covered in blood...

Liam Fallows (11)
St Bede CE Primary School, Bolton

Mushroom Manic

Starving, tired, Evie ran across the stream with a bunch of apples in her hand. While she was running, Evie dropped the apples. she couldn't get them back because she was being chased. The people who were chasing her picked them up and went back to the village.

Evie's belly started to rumble while she was walking. All of a sudden, Evie found a mushroom. She picked it and ate it. Then something weird started happening. She became a fox. she tried to get back to normal but it didn't work.

Mazie Ruby Louise Hall (11)

St Bede CE Primary School, Bolton

Shadows In The Forest

I was running through the forest. Something was chasing me. It looked like some sort of shadow... I looked to my right and saw an abandoned church. I ran into it and locked the door behind me. The shadow man was trying to get in.

All of a sudden, I saw some sort of floating, glowing ball, like a fairy. It buzzed, hinting at me to follow it, so I did. It led me to a mysterious portal. As the shadow man burst through the doors, I stepped in...

I suddenly woke up in bed. "What a weird dream!"

Ellen Kinney (10)
St Bride's Primary School, Belfast

The End

Leaves tumultuously crunched under my feet while the wind vigorously howled in my face. Confidently, I grabbed the straps of my backpack as I wandered.

Trees cast shadows on the moonlit paths, while darkness took me in like a mother hugging her child. I was getting nearer.

Alone, just me and nature. My tilted head faced upwards towards the stars, mesmerised. Not a soul was in sight. With each progressive step, I got closer.

At the cliff's edge, my head rounded as the minuscule village lay before me.

Deeply absorbing an immense breath... I icily whispered, "Home..."

Kalya Musial (11)
St Luke's CE Primary School, Lambeth

Lost In The Woods

It was getting dark. I was still lost. My heart started to pound as I started to run through the creeping trees faster. I heard a sudden crack. My heart stopped.

"H-hello? Is anyone there?"

I heard a growl.

"Argh!" I screamed as I started running faster than I had ever run before.

"Hello, little one," said a voice, echoing around the forest.

"What do you want from me?" I shouted, looking up.

Because I was looking up, I didn't realise there was a tree in front of me. I fell unconscious. I don't remember waking up...

Elsie Christine Ellis (10)

Sutton St James Primary School, Sutton St James

A Wander In The Woods

I heard a noise behind me. My skin began to crawl. My pulse started racing. Could this be the famous ghost of Stonebridge graveyard? I wasn't sure I believed in ghosts, however, alone in the graveyard on Halloween evening, maybe I was about to.

As quick as a flash, I turned to see... nothing. There wasn't anything there, whatever it was that made that screaming noise. With nervous steps, I began moving towards the church door. At that moment, the door began slowly creaking open.

Was I alone as I'd first thought or was the ghost of Stonebridge really real?

Ellis Redden (10)

Sutton St James Primary School, Sutton St James

Almost There

I'd escaped. I ran and ran as fast as I could. If I stopped, I'd be caught. The only place of escape was the Playground of Pain. I'd no choice but to go through there.

The place I'd escaped from was a daunting prison. They starved prisoners, so escaping was worth it. The muscular guards were still pursuing me. They were armed with steel, bulletproof handcuffs and tasers with a shock like lightning.

There it was! The Playground of Pain, the main exit out of here. I ran faster this time, but the gate slammed shut. I was suddenly surrounded...

Kasey Taylor (10)

Sutton St James Primary School, Sutton St James

The Mission

I arrived at the secret meeting place in the clearing of the eerie woods. The leaves crunched beneath my feet. I startled myself as a branch suddenly snapped. My heart beat even faster, like a hummingbird. The sun was visible through a tiny gap in the mass of branches above me.

"You made it, Lord Armaroon. We are so happy to see you!"

"Yes!" I said. "The mission was tough but I made it back alive, and with the princess safe and well. You must take over now and return her to the castle. The whole kingdom misses her."

Ryan Bollons (10)
Sutton St James Primary School, Sutton St James

The Horrifying Thought

"There must be a way out of here," said Josh, while sitting under his desk, frightened and feeling very lonely.

It all began when Josh found out the teacher was actually an alien from outer space, trying to take control of all the children one by one. Josh was the only child who hadn't been controlled by the alien and he was determined to make things right. Suddenly, there was a loud bang which woke Josh up. He felt relieved to discover it was all a dream. But, in the sky was a spaceship. What could that mean?

Kirk Barker (10)
Sutton St James Primary School, Sutton St James

The Dragon Chase

It was getting dark so I had to find shelter fast. It's unsafe out when it gets dark because of the dragons.

I'd only just found out that I was being chased by the dragons. All three dragons breathed fire all at once. They almost got me until I climbed a volcano.

The dragons went away and left me on the volcano. I started to climb down but... *boom!* A massive puddle of lava surrounded the volcano and myself, so I couldn't get down. Rocks tumbled down and into the lava. That was close!
Oh no...!

Leon (10)
Sutton St James Primary School, Sutton St James

Disappearing Exit

There must be a way out. I was lost, lost in the shaded woods. There was no time to stop moving. Something was chasing me. Twigs snapped. Leaves crunched. People screamed in pain. I saw an exit. The only problem was there was a caution sign. It read: 'Graveyard of gore...'
A shock shot through my heart. Bones lay on the floor and a rotten smell lingered as I took a step on the bloodstained bones.
I had to get out, quickly! I sprinted as fast as I could but there was no sign of the magical disappearing exit...

Leah Barker (11)
Sutton St James Primary School, Sutton St James

A Wander In The Woods

In a forest, a boy approached a door and entered without knowing the consequences...

The door shut and disappeared into the mist. A scream echoed through the land. Some goblins appeared. As he ran from the goblins, more appeared from the darkness. He ran to a house that was protected by a forcefield.

He found his siblings, who were already in this realm and told them to go into the house, grab the magic book and burn it. The goblins were looking for it and if they got it, the boy and his siblings would all die.

Zuzanna Poznaniak (11)

Sutton St James Primary School, Sutton St James

The Labyrinth

I'm Percy Jackson and I'm trying to escape the labyrinth. There must be a way out of this ancient maze made by Dedalus.
Suddenly, there were whispers.
"Don't say anything," Annabeth said.
She put her invisibility cap on. There was a half-dog, half-human figure. I went in and hid in a cart. When they found me, I grabbed Riptide and ran into the volcano. When I got in, I got zapped by Annabeth. In the end, I made an explosion. I ended up on an island with a girl. But not forever.

Aaron Martin (10)
Sutton St James Primary School, Sutton St James

A Wander In The Woods

I heard a noise behind me. It wasn't just any noise. It was a wail. A wail of despair. I turned around to see if they needed help, but there was no one there. I was confused. There definitely was a wail. I walked further to see if the noise had come from anywhere else.

As I approached the end of the street, the wail got louder. It seemed to be coming from a large mansion. I'd never seen it before. I went in and saw a little girl crying. I strolled towards her. Clearly, it was a mistake...

Aarav Keshvara (11)

Sutton St James Primary School, Sutton St James

A Wander In The Woods

Once upon a time, my friend and I were in the dark, horrible forest. We stumbled across three massive pandas and one baby panda.

When we travelled to the forest, at first, we fell into a hole. We discovered that it was a home for the pandas.

While we were both trying to find a way out, a panda came.

It said, "Hi, I see you have found our home."

We said, "Yes, we fell in. Can you let us out, please?

We heard something we never thought we would hear...

Zac Parker (10)

Sutton St James Primary School, Sutton St James

Dead!

It was getting dark. It was a late night in Hunter's Village. Two little children were settling into their beds when... *bang!*
"What was that, Sid?"
"I don't know, Rose. But it definitely went bang!"
"Well, yeah! We need to see what it was."
"Okay."
As they walked out to the woods, they saw something in the distance. It looked white. It was white but it had knives. Rose fell to the floor...

T B (9)
Sutton St James Primary School, Sutton St James

Is It A Dog Or Is It A Cat?

In the distance, I saw a dog creeping up on me, trying to get my attention. But why? It got closer until it was only a few feet away. Was it a dog or was it something else? It was grey and white.
I thought maybe it wasn't a dog. Maybe it was a cat because I'd never seen a dog like that before. It was small and had tiny ears. I picked it up and took it to the closest vets.
It was a tiny fox...

Elizabeth Norman (9)
Sutton St James Primary School, Sutton St James

The Field Of Fear

I heard a crack.

"Who's there?" I shouted, my voice echoing across the field.

There was no reply. I must have been hearing things.

As I carried on walking, I heard it again, but this time, it sounded closer. I froze. Someone was stalking me. I quickly turned around. No one was there...

Alesha Harrison (11)

Sutton St James Primary School, Sutton St James

The Blue Gemstone

Her feet crunched on beautiful, orange, autumn leaves as she wandered through the bright, colourful forest, searching for something to catch her attention. The girl's boots made a noise like sloshing water around a small pond, as she squelched through mud that had appeared after a rainstorm the night before. The evening sun glistened, sending rays sparkling in every direction. All at once, the adventurous girl saw a twinkle in the corner of her eye and ran over to a small log. She had found a wonderfully coloured blue gemstone! She got up and searched some more.

Elsie Freegard (11)
Tangmere Primary Academy, Tangmere

A Wander In The Woods

I entered the outrageous forest. My sister and I saw some dragons above the trees. The forest was completely dead. My sister saw a megalodon eating a whale in the sea in this magical place. Later, we saw the megalodon sobbing.

It shouted, "The star, Betelgeuse, is going to explode and the creatures will die in this forest." My sister was scared of the megalodon, but I hugged him.

All of a sudden, the star exploded, but all the creatures survived.

We celebrated with a massive party. My sister and I had an amazing time in the outrageous forest!

Matvey Avetisyan (8)

The Academy School, Rosslyn Hill

A Wander In The Woods

One day, five children went camping in the woods. Night fell upon them so they built a fire, but they had built it on an ancient burial ground!

Just then, two spirits, an angel and a devil floated up from the ground. One of the children, called Ava, was taken over by both spirits!

One night, the devil said to Ava, "You know, your angel side isn't very fun!"

The next night, the angel said, "You know, the devil is bad!"

Ava agreed.

The spirit police were called and they arrested the devil.

Ava lived happily forever.

Saoirse Leech (8)

The Academy School, Rosslyn Hill

A Wander In The Woods

It was getting dark, but I knew I had to do this. I entered the mysterious wood at the end of my garden.

Suddenly, there was a bang and a flash. It was a scarlet-horned cobra! I ducked behind a bush and quickly read the scarlet-horned cobra section of the animal book that I'd bought with me. Then I took my torch and shone it in the snake's wicked eyes. It slithered away.

I went home. I would never again go to the haunted wood.

Lily Husain (8)
The Academy School, Rosslyn Hill

Little Blue Riding Hood

Once upon a time, there was Little Blue Riding Hood. She lived alone because three wolves attacked her whole family. She was really sad but she was used to not seeing her family because they all worked all day.

She went to Weeping Woods to find the wolves. But she got unlucky every time so she went every day. She only saw goats, horses and deer. She cried and cried.

But one day, she saw the three wolves. She pulled out a double-barrelled shotgun. She knocked out two of the wolves and then killed the other one.

Romeo Tomlinson (8)

The Bewbush Academy, Bewbush

The Ghost Valley

I heard a noise behind me. I turned. Nothing. Now another. Again, nothing. I stood up and started to run.

In the gloomy shadows of the trees, I saw sinister glowing red eyes. Suddenly, *crack!* The sound shocked me so much I tripped. I heard whispers as I hit the ground hard. I got up, trembling, and carried on running.

A barbaric wind blew, making me shiver. Was my friend right? Was this place... No, it wasn't possible.

I felt alone in the darkness. I saw a light. Was I alone or not...?

Ella Hoelters (9)
The Bewbush Academy, Bewbush

Five Fairies

I arrived at the meeting place. I saw five fairies sitting on diamond mushrooms that glimmered in the ruby sunset. We were waiting for it...

Suddenly, there was a rustle in the bushes. But it was a false alarm. Then... *snap!* The twigs broke like rocks crashing into the sea. But it was only the owl.

They waited and waited. They played games and ate lunch.

Days came and went and they found nothing.

One morning, the twigs snapped. It was the fox and he wasn't alone...

Victoria Dragan (8)

The Bewbush Academy, Bewbush

The Death Of Harry Potter

Harry Potter and Hermione went through the woods. The woods were haunted. Harry Potter and Hermione were looking for the spy in an old haunted house from 1980.

When Harry Potter went to the toilet, the spy killed him. When Hermione went to the toilet, she saw Harry Potter dead. She screamed so loud. She cried so much. Then the spy killed Hermione in the bathroom.

The spy was mad, so he killed everyone who went to his home.

No one went to his home again.

Lilly-Grace Bowden (8)
The Bewbush Academy, Bewbush

Lost

It was getting dark, three children were lost in the woods, they found a creature. They then heard a noise behind them, it was so creepy and scary, the three children ran away out of the woods.
They ran back home to their parents. The three children went to sleep in their beds.
In the middle of the night, the noise came back, The three kids ran out of the house, Moon, Sammy and Sara were scared.

Sasha Neill (9)
The Bewbush Academy, Bewbush

A Wander In The Woods

Once upon a time, a girl called Maisie and a boy called Tom went to the woods.

"Is it going to be dark?" asked Maisie.

"Of course!" replied Tom.

They went into the woods.

"Woah, this is creepy," shivered Maisie.

"Watch out, there's a bat!" Tom said, creeped out.

"Hi!" squeaked the bat.

"Hi! I'm Maisie, this is Tom," replied Maisie.

"Hi!" said Tom.

"I'm Batasha," replied the bat.

"We're going for a walk," Tom said.

"Be careful, kids!" said Batasha.

"Do you want to come?" asked Maisie.

"Yes!" said Batasha.

They went for a walk. Batasha became their pet!

Viola Tammaro (8)

Yattendon School, Horley

Emily And The Monster

An evil monster, called Scaramolt, would appear in a village and kill all the people, children, cats and dogs.

The king announced, "Whoever can defeat this beat will get a reward."

Wizards and witches came and went. Some were turned evil and some were killed.

In the end, a young girl, called Emily, went to the king.

"How will you kill the monster without an adult?" shouted the king.

"I have a spell that he'll not forget in a hurry!"

Emily found Scaramolt in his cave and used her unforgettable spell to defeat him and saved the village.

Millie Finch (7)

Yattendon School, Horley

Sunny Black And The Seven Tall People

In an ancient castle, a girl named Sunny Black lived with her mother. Sunny's poorly mother had an illness called Mirrorlites. Sunny had no choice but to leave her mother, otherwise, she would catch the illness and never be able to leave home! Sunny packed her stuff and said goodbye to her mother. She headed off into the distance. Sunny wandered around the enchanted woods and saw a lovely ornate cottage surrounded by patches of beautiful sunflowers. Sunny peeked through the stained glass window and saw seven tall people. Netty, Footy, Golfy, Tenny, Baskty, Cricky and Rugby...

Lily Bartlett (11)
Yattendon School, Horley

The Genie's Adventure Awaits

Once upon a time, there was a castle with two special people, two genies. There was a queen, her name was Bethany, and the king's name was Alex. They ruled the city together.

One day, a citizen came and said, "Everyone is getting poorly. We need more medicine."

Alex and Bethany went into the forest. They looked everywhere for the healing plant. They went into a cave and found it.

They went back to the city and gave it to the hospitals. Everyone got better.

"Thank you, you really are the best!"

Everyone lived well and happily.

Chloe Pickett (7)

Yattendon School, Horley

The Gnomealeague

The wolves walked towards the opponents. Both teams were part of the Gnomaleague, the best league in history.

Kyle Runner, the best player in the land, walked onto the pitch, clapping his opponents. The ref blew the whistle and the match started.

Kyle went in for a slide tackle against Paul Poles. He won the ball and ran towards the goal. He shot and scored. But nobody cheered. The crowd were not bothered anymore he had scored that many times!

Kyle walked off the pitch into the dressing room in the trees. Why were the crowd not bothered anymore?

Jake Bardsley (11) & Charlie George (11)
Yattendon School, Horley

Moonlight

As the autumn leaves rustled in the wind and the trees waved their goodbyes, I stepped through the ivy-covered door. All at once, I landed on a broken branch. When I looked up, the glowing moon beamed down upon the diamond river. The sky was a misty black, making all the animals stand out.

Suddenly, sky-blue butterflies and rose-gold ladybirds fluttered around the sky, making the night even more magical. Two deer then came up to me, their chocolate-brown face and snow-white spots glowing. The branches were a musky silver... a magical silver.

Olivia Harding (10)

Yattendon School, Horley

Meeting With Death

I arrived at the secret meeting place. As soon as I
had looked around, I felt quite worried. The area
was entirely deserted and bird carcasses
decorated the forest floor. The red feathers on my
belly blew in the eerie wind and my wings were
clamped tight to my sides.

A thick mist hung over the leaf-covered ground. I
sprang around when I heard rustling behind me. I
shivered in fright as a snarling fox came towards
me, his muscles flexing as he walked. His eyes
glinted greedily as his claws swung in my direction.
Suddenly, I knew no more...

Freya Hawley (10)
Yattendon School, Horley

A Wander In The Woods

It was getting dark, Jess was bored so she went to the forbidden woods.
When she got there, she realised that she shouldn't have gone in. Jess tried to turn back but there was no way out. Jess ran straight ahead.
Suddenly, she bumped into something. It was big, green and disgusting. It was a troll with a big bat. Jess tried to run away but he caught her.
"Help!" she shouted.
A big owl came. The owl swooped past the troll and grabbed the bat. It smacked the troll on the head.
Jess woke up. It was a dream!

Madeleine Birch (9)
Yattendon School, Horley

Jimmy Hill's Adventure

Jimmy Hill was a footballer.

One day, he found a magical ball, which was gold and silver. He picked it up and there was a teleporter.

He went in and couldn't believe it! It teleported him and to the past and he could see dinosaurs! He trained, hiding and looking for food to eat. Finally, he wanted to go back home.

Jimmy Hill found the same ball, but this time, he saw a button. He pressed it and he arrived at a football pitch. All the practice paid off because he played in the final.

He won because he'd practised!

Ollie Luszczak (7)

Yattendon School, Horley

The Race For The Jewel Of Nakamu

I'd escaped the Pyramid of Giza and was going to my rusty helicopter when a pack of leopards started chasing me.

My name is AJ. I'm twelve and I'm now in a helicopter with a ninety-year-old flying it. I'm at Nakamu. Pete Rogers is here too. We're going to have to race for the jewel.

I'm in Nakamu pyramid and am entering the lava and acid room. I swing over that and am running past spikes and racing past mummies. I'm at the top, but Pete is already there. He grabs the cursed jewel and he slowly melts...

Coby Jones (11)
Yattendon School, Horley

School Escape

I arrived at the secret meeting place. It was dark outside and I was the first to arrive.

We discussed our plans together over biscuits and lemonade.

After that, I went home and back to bed.

In the morning, I thought about our plans with a nervous knot in my tummy.

At school, the time to carry out our plan drew closer. As the long, snaking line disappeared around the corner at breaktime. The five of us climbed quickly over the wall and dropped onto the grass. We grinned at each other in relief. But what to do next?

Oliver Challis (8)
Yattendon School, Horley

Good Deed

Long ago in the woods, there were two people called Sophia and Ryan. They went into the woods to build a den. Once they had built it, they found a puppy with no owner. Sophia recalled seeing a lost puppy poster.

They made their way to the poster to find the phone number to call the owner. Eureka! It was the same dog and there was a £100 reward.

An hour later, the puppy was returned home. They didn't want the reward money. their reward was seeing the pup's tail wagging with happiness when it saw the owner.

Sophia Graham (9)
Yattendon School, Horley

Lost

It was getting dark. I was lost. I needed somewhere to stay. Then I found a forest. *I guess this is better than nothing*, I thought.

I made my way into the woods. There was a campfire. Someone else was there. I didn't want to stay. I ran.

I ran as far away as I could. Then I tripped. I fell down a hill.

"More light?"

There was a house. I thought I had no choice but to knock, so I did. There were footsteps coming towards the door. The door opened. I wasn't prepared for what I saw...

Caitlin Jobson (10)
Yattendon School, Horley

Alex And The Giant

There once was a girl called Alex. She got a necklace from her grandma for her birthday. Alex put the necklace on and began to feel dizzy. She fell to the floor.

Alex woke up in a place that she had never seen before. She got up and heard a small voice. It was a little monkey. She got really scared.

There was a rumble. The whole land moved. They both got up and ran for their lives. Behind them, there was a massive giant chasing them. It was terrifying. They hid behind a bush.

What will happen next...?

Esme Lyon-Lee (10)

Yattendon School, Horley

Sammy The Sea Otter

Once upon a time, there lived a sea otter named Sammy.

One day, he swam to the bottom of the ocean and picked up a rock. He took it back up to the surface with some shellfish. He used the rock to smash the shellfish. This was when he realised he'd turned invisible.

As he tucked into his shellfish, he heard a distant call from a fish. He swam over to see what was going on. The fish was being attacked by a great white shark.

A moment later, Sammy made himself invisible so he could rescue the fish.

Teddy King (8)

Yattendon School, Horley

The Nearby Castle

It was getting dark, I needed to get home. I noticed that home was ten miles away. I couldn't get home very fast.

I found a nearby castle. I went into the castle and found magical things like talking animals and flying pigs!

Suddenly, the gates closed. I jumped. I was scared. I needed to find a way out. I jumped in surprise when I saw the flying pig pass behind me. I was really worried about my family. Then I thought of the flying pig... I could hop on it and fly home...

Olivia Moore (9)
Yattendon School, Horley

The Graveyard

It was getting dark and cold. The rain started to turn into hailstones the size of golf balls. I ran towards the old, ruined church.

In the distance, there was an old man dressed in what looked like a clown outfit, covered in bright red blood. He was wandering around the graveyard with a bloody, long, rusty knife in his hand.

I was spooked out because I thought in my mind, that he had seen me. I needed to focus on my plan to escape and not get distracted by 'him'!

Sophia Williams (10)

Yattendon School, Horley

The Den

Once upon a time, a little girl and her sister set off into the woods where they hadn't been before. It was a cold night so they built a den and slept in it. In the morning, they went further into the wood and found a rope swing and a house made of sticks. They went to find some fish.

They set a fire and cooked the fish. They found some fish that looked like knives and forks and plates. They ate the fish and lived in the woods forever!

Fleur Hunt (7)

Yattendon School, Horley

Shquan

As I entered the woods, I felt a chill down my spine and my blood froze. A blanket of dense mist covered the wet, slimy floor. Ravens filled the sky. Finally, I found the river Sami. The water was scarlet-red. Then I saw it... the Shquan. It had amber scales and razor-sharp teeth. I held my diamond sword up to it. The Shquan rose out of the water. Its sheer size towered over me. Its crimson eyes locked onto me and then it attacked...

Nicholas Lowes (11)
Yattendon School, Horley

Scary Things At Night

I heard a noise behind me. I didn't know what it was. It was late at night and I was on my own. My mum and dad were back at the cabin and my sister was too.

As the noise got closer, it jumped out at me. It was my sister. She was way older than me. She came to take me back to the cabin.

My mum, dad, sister and I all sat down and had biscuits and tea. Then my sister told my parents I had been scared.

Bea Millard (10)
Yattendon School, Horley

YOUNG WRITERS INFORMATION

We hope you have enjoyed reading this book – and that you will continue to in the coming years.

If you're a young writer who enjoys reading and creative writing, or the parent of an enthusiastic poet or story writer, visit our website **www.youngwriters.co.uk/subscribe** to join the World of Young Writers and receive news, competitions, writing challenges, tips, articles and giveaways! There is lots to keep budding writers motivated to write!

If you would like to order further copies of this book, or any of our other titles, then please give us a call or order via your online account.

Young Writers
Remus House
Coltsfoot Drive
Peterborough
PE2 9BF
(01733) 890066
info@youngwriters.co.uk

Join in the conversation!
Tips, news, giveaways and much more!

 YoungWritersUK    @YoungWritersCW    @YoungWritersCW